Ellora's Cave Publishin

Discover for yourself why readers can't
of the multiple award-winning publish
Cave. Whether you prefer e-books or p
be sure to visit EC on the
www.ellorascave.com for an eroti
experience that will leave you breathless

www.ellorascave.co

ense and action filled, hot enough to burn
. This one will particularly appeal to female
being sexually dominated. Jaid Black in her
– *Pandora's Box on the Death Row serial*

DEATH ROW:

THE FUGITIVE

Written by

Jaid Black

ve Publishing, Inc.

H 44236-0787

1360-367-5

ow: The Fugitive, Jaid Black, 2001

Cris Brashear.
y Novella Studios.

The following material contains strong
tent meant for mature readers. *Death
ugitive* has been rated NC17, erotic, by
endent reviewers. We strongly suggest
; book in a place where young readers
to view it are unlikely to happen upon it.
enjoy…

To MT & Walmart…
It'll NEVER happen, babe ;)

"If the first woman God ever made was strong enough to turn the world upside down alone, these women together ought to be able to turn it back, and get it right side up again."

— *Sojourner Truth*

Prologue

MY BELOVED KERICK,

HOW I GRIEVE FOR YOU...FOR ALL THAT YOU HAVE LOST AND FOR ALL THAT YOU WILL CONTINUE TO LOSE AS YOU GROW INTO MANHOOD. WHY COULDN'T LIFE HAVE DEALT US A BETTER HAND, MY SON?

BUT WHEN ALL IS SAID AND DONE, IT STILL COMES DOWN TO THIS: THERE IS NO UTILITY IN WISHING FOR A DIFFERENT LIFE, NOR IS THERE ANY USE IN DREAMING OF A HAPPY ENDING.

THERE IS ONLY THE REALITY OF OUR EXISTENCE AND THE REALITY OF OUR NEED TO SURVIVE.

MARGARET RILEY,
DECEMBER 24, 2216

Chapter 1

Cell Block 29:
Death Row unit within the Kong Penal Colony.
40 miles outside the Mayan pyramidal ruins of Altun Ha
in former Belize, The United Americas of Earth,
December 17, 2249 A.D.

"Prisoner, Riley. Remove your clothing."

Kerick Riley's dark head came up slowly, his cold gray eyes flicking dispassionately over the smirking face of the prison warden. Wiping mud from his eyes, he rose up to his feet from the pen of wet dirt and blood he'd been kicked into, simultaneously noting everything there was to see about the executioner. From the pristine white silk robe the warden wore, to the flash-stick in his hand that could ignite and thereby sizzle a man to death at mere contact, nothing escaped his notice.

For fifteen years, seven months, three weeks, and five days, Kerick had waited with an inhuman patience for the arrival of this moment. He'd never allowed his mental acumen or extreme physical strength to lessen from lack of use over the years, that both would be there to serve him when the hour of reckoning had at last come upon him.

It had worked — it *would* work.

Never once in all of those fifteen plus years had he allowed his thoughts to betray him. He knew when it was safe to think, and he knew as well when it was necessary to create a void in his mind to prohibit a detection scanner from probing what went on in his thoughts.

From a young age he had been taught the necessity of control, his mother having gone so far as to beat the lessons into him. She'd used such harsh tactics not because she had hated her son, but conversely because she had adored him, and more fundamentally, because she had wanted him to live.

The lessons in bodily and mental control passed down from Margaret Riley had done more than help Kerick survive in the violent world of twenty-third century Earth; they had also made it possible for him to survive this day. Today. The dwindling hours of remaining daylight prior to his execution.

Kerick's sharp gray eyes continued to study the warden, but betrayed none of his emotions. They simply calculated and assessed with an almost robotic precision, doing the same as they'd always done these past fifteen years. He realized that the sadistic warden had always despised — and envied — his ability to think and behave as though he were a machine, for it made predicting his behavior impossible.

Warden Jallor tapped the flash-stick against his thigh, his eyebrows shooting up mockingly. He believed he'd won, Kerick knew, thought indeed that the prisoner was about to die…

But—no.

For nearly every waking moment of the past fifteen years, Kerick had calculated, assessed, plotted, and planned. He had noted the weaknesses of the 50-story structure surrounding him, had made certain that he'd learned all there was to know of the seemingly impenetrable fortress that was his prison. For the most part, he understood that Warden Jallor was correct—Kong was an impenetrable fortress. But Kerick also understood that there was no such thing as invincible, and he had spent fifteen years learning how to defeat the undefeatable Kong.

Officially entitled Correctional Sector 12, the penal colony of Kong had gotten its nickname from an old black-and-white movie none from Kerick's time had ever seen but all had heard tell of. It was said that in the old movie the god-like ape King Kong could escape from any prison, but not even the Mighty Kong could escape Sector 12. For most prisoners, that statement turned out to be chillingly true, but for Kerick Riley…

"Remove your clothes," Warden Jallor snapped, his patience nearing an end. His icy blue eyes flicked down to the innocuous bulge in the prisoner's pants. "Now."

He wanted to kill him. For year after bitter year, Kerick had comforted himself with thoughts of Jallor's death, with thoughts of avenging himself—and avenging his mother. But for the moment at least, such was not to be. He needed the warden alive. For now.

But when it was over, when all was said and done...

Kerick's stoic gaze never wavered from Jallor's as he slowly, methodically, removed first his prison-issued woolen tunic and finally his woolen pants. Both garments were a dirty, muted brown, filthy and greasy from having been worn for three solid years without a cleaning. In truth, removing the disgusting clothing was practically a relief. It would mean he was naked during the escape, but so be it.

When he was finished, Kerick stood before Warden Jallor in stone-faced silence, his heavily muscled six-foot five-inch frame completely divested of clothing, his brooding eyes that saw everything piercing the warden's.

Jallor's gaze wandered down to Kerick's penis, then back up to his face.

He was a stupid man, Kerick knew. Sadistic but stupid. Removing the prisoner from his chains would prove to be his downfall.

With the sensory chains on, Kerick never would have stood a chance at escaping. The moment he ventured outside the perimeter of the Kong penal colony, the sensors within the chains would have detonated and his skin would have gone up in flames, charring him to ashes within seconds.

But on the day of execution the chains were removed — the only day in a Death Row inmate's life where that was so.

Warden Jallor stepped towards him, careful to keep his distance, his smirk deepening. "Fifteen years ago you swore this day would never come to pass," he said in a mocking tone. "Indeed, how the mighty have fallen."

For the first time in fifteen years, Kerick smiled — a gesture that caused the warden to frown. "Yes," Kerick agreed, his deep rumble of a voice scratchy from a prolonged lack of use, "how the mighty have fallen."

Two guards appeared behind Jallor. The warden made a dismissive motion with his head, indicating it was time to retreat and step aside while the flash-stick was detonated. The warden barely had time to gasp before the flash-stick was snatched from his hand, rendering him completely defenseless from an assault.

"What are you doing?" Jallor snapped at one of the guards, his eyes promising retribution. "Hand the weapon over and take your place at the—"

The warden's words came to a halt when the "guard" holding the flash-stick peeled off his face armor. Jallor gulped as he looked up into the grim ebony face of Elijah Carter, a Death Row inmate who was scheduled to be executed next week.

Kerick walked slowly towards Jallor. His jaw tightened as he came to a stop before him, staring down at the wide-eyed warden. With a growl he picked Jallor up off of the ground by the neck, his grip tightening until the warden's throat began to elicit gurgling sounds.

"Don't kill him," Elijah warned. "Not yet." He glanced over to the secret panel in the execution pen that allowed for a magistrate of justice to escape should situations like this one ever arise. That panel would take them to the outermost perimeter of Kong. From there, Kerick, Elijah, and Xavier would be on their own in the jungle. "The DNA scanner only responds to living flesh prints, amigo."

"You sure?" Kerick snarled.

"As sure as I can be."

Kerick grunted, but said nothing. He tightened his hold on the warden's neck fractionally, letting Jallor know he'd never allow him to live once they'd gotten from him the palm scan they sought.

"We need the bitch alive," Elijah reminded him.

Nostrils flaring, Kerick turned his head and stared hard at Elijah. Seeing his familiar face, and realizing as he did that Elijah would be executed next week if they were caught, he regained his sanity long enough to let loose of his hold on the sadistic warden.

Jallor gasped when Kerick released his throat. He panted for air as he fell to the ground and turned eyes filled with hatred on the prisoner-turned-executioner.

Kerick smiled slowly, his steel gray eyes locking with the warden's. "Indeed," he murmured, "How the mighty have fallen."

Chapter 2

Altun Ha, former Belize
December 19, 2249 A.D.

"Shit." A beleaguered Nellie Kan ran a hand through her sweat-drenched hair and sighed. She turned to the Spanish-speaking guard of Fathom Systems, Inc. and attempted to converse with him using what little of the language she'd managed to acquire while living and working in the Belizean sector these past two years.

Back when the sector had been its own nation the prominent tongue of the people living here had been English, but that had changed a few decades past when Belize had become federated within the United Americas of Earth colony. "Que le paso al sistema de ventilacción?" she asked in a thick accent. *What has happened to the ventilation system?*

Christ! she grumbled to herself for the thousandth time in two years, was it too much to ask of the mega-conglomerate company to provide air within the Altun Ha biosphere for its scientists and other workers? Apparently it was, for she had put the same question to the same guard at least three times a week for as long as she'd lived and worked within the synthetic black glass dome known officially as Biosphere 77.

She took a deep breath and blew it out. She really needed a vacation.

"Doctor Kan, voy a ver lo que pueda hacer antes de irme esta noche," Juan promised on a grin. *I'll go see what I can do before I leave for the night, Doctor Kan.* Juan was as accustomed to having this conversation as Nellie was. "Te digo buenas noches." *I bid you goodnight.*

Nellie smiled at the aging guard as he turned and walked away, the flash-stick in his hand absently thumping against his armor-encased thigh as he strolled from the sealed chamber whistling to himself. She watched him for a moment or two before turning back to the virtual reality display module she was currently working with, then settled back in her seat to resume her research.

Three more weeks, she thought excitedly, her heartbeat thumping against her chest as her fingers flicked over the keyboard. At the rate she was acquiring data, she would be able to produce a test serum from a randomly sampled control group of sub-humans within three weeks time.

She refused to consider the possibility that Boris Karli, her chief rival at Fathom Systems, might beat her to the punch and develop a serum first. She was aware of the fact that the lying, manipulative son-of-a-defective-droid had been thumbing through her notes on the sly, but she doubted that he had enough ingenuity to do anything with them.

If Boris defied expectations and developed a serum, well then, the more power to him. Nellie's goal was to ease the suffering of sub-humans. Dr. Karli's goal was and had always been fame and notoriety — preferably attained with as little work as possible.

Which was why Nellie doubted he'd figure out even the basics to a serum. He was one of those types of males who thought he knew everything, yet understood very little. The serum, she realized, was up to her.

And when it was done, when she had found the answers she was seeking, she would be careful, of course, to never break her word to the older, infected woman who had given her the dusty, worn-out diary that had proven to be a vital aide...and chillingly accurate.

Nellie would never tell anyone — *anyone* — that the basis of her entire research was derived from the journal of one Dr. Margaret Riley. To do so would mean not only academic suicide, but it could also mean...

Well, she wouldn't think on that.

In life, the discredited Dr. Riley had been branded a heretic by her scientific peers. In death, she was still regarded as heretical, though there were those who whispered behind closed doors that perhaps — *perhaps*...

Perhaps Dr. Riley hadn't been as insane as the Hierarchy would lead people to believe she had been.

Her ideas had been...bizarre. And because of the oddity of them, because of the fact they had seemed too fantastical, too completely unbelievable, they had been systematically dismissed as the delusions of a paranoid schizophrenic. That schizophrenia had been cured and done away with decades ago...well, no scientist would have dared to bring *that* reminder up to her accusers in order to defend the outspoken heretic known as Dr. Margaret Riley. Not if they had aspirations for waking up alive the next morning. That nobody had seemed to know exactly *who* the doctor's accusers were was proof positive it was a stone best left unturned.

Too hot and sweaty to concentrate on her work, Nellie sighed as her hands fell from the keyboard and she slumped further into the chair. She ran a hand through her dark red hair, absently reminding herself it was time to get a hair shearing. A low-maintenance female scientist, she preferred to keep her hair cropped short so she didn't have to mess with it. That she'd allowed it to grow so long was a sure sign of how immersed she'd been in her research as of late.

When the air in the laboratory grew too heavy and oppressive for her to remain inside, she took a deep breath to keep from passing out, then stood up. Parting the heavy woolen robe she was wearing into a wide vee, Nellie removed the thick article of body décor, allowing it to fall to the ground and cascade in a puddle around her feet. Naked, she padded across the lab chamber toward a storage closet, her goal to find a sheer robe or pantsuit she could don long enough to reach her domicile.

"Oh come on," she muttered to herself as she rummaged through the storage closet. She parted three woolen lab suits that had been slung haphazardly on cheap hangars to see if any sheerer body décors were hanging behind them. "There has to be—"

She stilled, the hair at the nape of her neck stirring. She swallowed nervously, recognizing the sensation she'd just experienced for what it was:

She was being watched. *Someone* was watching her.

Nellie closed her eyes briefly as she steeled herself to remain calm, realizing as she did just who that someone was. She could feel her heart rate betraying her, but she'd undergone enough detection scans in her life to realize when her mental and bodily reactions were being probed for answers and when they weren't. She felt no nausea, no cramping in her mind, so she knew she was safe. For now.

And now she also understood why the ventilation system was no longer working. She had, after all, been through this routine almost as many times as she'd been through the "what's happened to the ventilation system" conversation she frequently had with Juan. Difference was, she hadn't been expecting this tonight, for Henders hadn't come into the lab all day long.

Reminding herself it was best just to play along, she bent over into the closet, pretending obliviousness to her employer's voyeurism as she took her time searching for a sheer lab suit. She knew just how to angle her body into a lean, knew how far apart to keep her ankles, so that Vorice Henders would be given an arousingly close-up view of the folds of flesh between her legs.

Perversely, she felt her body respond to the knowledge it was being watched. She realized, however, that the tightening of her nipples and the saturation between her legs wasn't being caused by Vorice Henders the man—it was being caused by the idea of knowing a man, even a man like Henders, was watching her in this way. A big difference.

Nellie took her time locating a sheer lab coat, giving her voyeuristic boss plenty of time to bring himself to completion while watching her. In a world where men took women at will—and often times against the women's will—she supposed giving Henders jack-off material was a small price to pay for her independence. She was protected within the biosphere, an accomplished scientist allowed to work for pay rather than be bound to a male for free, and that's all that mattered. For now.

Still feigning obliviousness, she turned around and offered the sensory cameras a full view of the front of her nude body. She allowed a confused frown to mar her face as she pretended to glance around, searching out other places where a sheer lab coat might be located.

Just then the ventilation system came on full blast, inducing Nellie to gasp when the chilled air hit her square in the face. Her rosy nipples immediately hardened and elongated, which she realized was what Henders had been hoping would happen. His office was located on the other side of the concourse, but she almost felt as though she could hear him gasping and groaning while he yanked his disgusting self off into oblivion.

She took a deep breath and blew it out. She really needed a vacation.

Nellie debated within herself as to what she should do for as long as she felt she could get away with it without arousing suspicion that she was clued in as to Henders' activities.

She could put on her body décor and retreat to her domicile—or she could finish this perverse little show, perhaps earning herself the right to be left alone for a month or more.

She decided on the latter.

Closing her eyes, she ran her hands over her breasts, her full lips parting slightly on a sigh as she began to massage her nipples. She used her thumbs and forefingers to latch onto the bases, gasping as she massaged upward to the tip of her nipples and back. She tried to pretend she was alone in her domicile and doing this for her own pleasure, for Henders was a vile, disgusting man, and it made her skin crawl to think about the fact that he was watching her do something so private and intimate.

It's best this way, Nellie, she reminded herself. *You need to finish that serum and Henders is your only protection from the others.*

Resolved, Nellie continued to massage her nipples as she hoisted herself up onto a nearby table and spread her thighs wide so her employer would get the best show possible. She was careful not to knock over any beakers as she settled atop the table, preparing to masturbate herself into orgasm.

She continued to toy with a plumped up nipple in one hand while her other hand began roaming downwards, over her lightly tanned belly, then lower still through the triangle of dark red curls pointing toward the flesh of her cunt. She could feel his eyes on her, devouring her, more intense than they'd ever watched her before...

Her fingers found the warm, wet flesh of her pussy. She moaned softly as she began running them through the sleek folds, spreading the puffy lips wide open for Henders' voyeuristic pleasure with the hand that had dropped from her breast. "Yes," she murmured, pretending she was alone, "yes."

Nellie gasped at the first touch of fingers to clit, the hedonistic sensations jolting through her not fabricated. She continued to pretend she was alone, then no longer cared if she was or wasn't when the pleasure grew in its intensity and she drew nearer to orgasm. "Oh god," she breathed out as her fingers briskly rubbed her clit in a circular motion. Her nipples jutted out as her head fell back and her eyes closed. "*Yes.*"

Panting heavily, she moaned as she masturbated herself faster, faster, and faster still. Her free hand came up and rubbed over her stiff nipples, then fell once more to her lap. On a groan she stuffed two fingers into her cunt, gasping and moaning as she finger-fucked herself with one hand and masturbated her clit with the other.

Blood rushed to her face to heat it. Blood coursed into her nipples, elongating them to the point of near pain. She could feel his eyes on her, the intensity of his stare more powerful than ever before…

"Oh god." She stifled a loud moan as she broke, contenting herself with a softer one. Gasping, she fucked herself as hard as she could with two fingers as the orgasm ripped through her belly in a tidal wave of sensation.

When it was over, when she'd given Henders his show, she fell onto her back, exhausted. From the angle of the cameras, she knew he couldn't see her face. All he could see was her body laying spread out on the table like a submissive offering, her nipples stabbing up into the air, the flesh of her cunt ripe and swollen from a recent and powerful orgasm. She laid there for a couple of minutes like that, panting until her breathing resumed its normal gait.

Deciding she'd given the perverted Henders more than enough time to jack himself off once or twice, she sat up slowly, then looked around for her woolen lab coat. It was still laying where she'd first dropped it, puddled in a heap on the floor next to her chair at the virtual reality display.

She felt the sensory cameras turn off as she walked over to where her lab coat lay, and she breathed a sigh of relief at realizing that the show was well and truly over for tonight. Her nostrils flared at the injustice of it all as she snatched the woolen robe up off of the ground.

It wasn't right—the horrid price all women had to pay for freedom. And, she thought bitterly, was freedom at such a steep price truly freedom at all?

If the world had been a different place two hundred years ago, if males hadn't been so highly valued over females, then couples wouldn't have rushed off to genetic specialists to make certain the babies they birthed were all males. The result a couple of generations later had equaled disaster, for the planet was now overrun with men, making it so females of all races and nationalities were very rare—and very expensive.

Nellie couldn't recall how many times she'd been verbally slandered in her thirty-two years for petitioning to the Hierarchy for the right to practice a career over being auctioned off for marriage. But she'd never permitted the negativity of others to thwart her from her goals, for she'd always known she was born to be a scientist. Hypothesizing and finding answers came to her as easily as breathing. Researching and experimentation was as natural to her as violence was to sub-humans...

Sub-humans, she reminded herself as she finished donning the woolen lab coat—she was their best hope for help for few other scientists seemed to care if they lived or died. If she had to endure Henders and his voyeurism for a bit longer in order to finish that serum, then she would. She had lost her own mother to infection. She wanted to save other children from the same fate that had for all intent and purposes orphaned her at age fourteen.

Ten minutes later, Nellie flicked off the virtual display screen and padded over toward the sliding sensory door, ignoring the sound of rushing air as it whisked open. With the same rushing air sound it closed behind her, now sealed off against anyone not possessing either her, Henders, or the guard Juan's DNA genetic map.

Walking quickly toward the airbus railway that would take her to the other side of the biosphere where she lived, she didn't pay much attention to her surroundings. She gasped a moment later when she walked head first into a man, her face hitting a solid wall of muscle.

"I'm so sorry," she offered in the way of apology, her head coming up to find the man's face. "I wasn't paying attention to…to…"

She swallowed a bit nervously when her large green eyes found his steely gray ones. They were so intense—frighteningly intense—that for a moment she feared a sub-human had broken into the biosphere. But when she considered that his eyes were steel gray as opposed to that haunting blood-red color, she knew she was letting her overactive imagination rot her brain. "I wasn't paying attention to where I was going," she finished breathily.

The man said nothing, which made her more nervous. He simply stared at her from under the cowled hood of his black robe, his intense eyes flicking over her face, and over her body. He was a big man, much bigger than her five foot seven inch frame, and broader across the shoulders than any man she'd ever before seen.

Nellie backed up a step. He was handsome, yes, but he was far too intense. And eerily quiet. "I have to be going," she said dumbly, uncertain what to do or say. She backed up another step as her eyes flicked over his chiseled masculine face. The rest of his features were as intense as his eyes—brooding lips, a hawk-like nose, an expression akin to chilled stone…

She turned and walked away from him, no longer caring if she came across as rude or not. The man frightened her. And given her family history, it took a lot to frighten Dr. Nellie Kan.

She could feel his intense eyes following her movement, like a predator tracking prey. She realized that he was still watching her, not needing to turn around and see him to confirm it. She walked faster, and faster still, desperate to reach the main atrium off the corridor where she knew she could lose herself in the crowd…

Footsteps. Slow and heavy at first, then quick and paced closer together.

Shit, she thought uneasily, the man was following her.

Nellie picked up the edges of her woolen robe and sprinted at top speed toward the corridor. The footfalls matched her pace, the sound of them getting closer and closer and —

She pushed open the heavy doors with an oomph, and bodily thrust herself into the atrium. She breathed easier, understanding as she did that males — even *that* male if he possessed a modicum of intelligence — would be less likely to ignore her protected status and claim her when others were around to view the illegal activity.

The doors fell shut behind her. The footfalls came to an abrupt halt.

A group of ten females, chained and naked brides-to-be, were led in a procession in front of her, preparing to be taken to the bathing chamber before being auctioned off in marriage to the highest bidder. A group of young males were gathering around to watch, their moods light and festive as they playfully tweaked at the nipples of the females passing by.

"Can't wait til I have enough yen to buy one," a blond teenager with a hard-on announced.

"Shit, me neither," another one laughed as he ran his fingers through a frightened bride-to-be's thatch of nether hair. "Cummon, Auctioneer Morris," he said to the man holding the females' chains, "can't I fuck this one before you take her off to the auction block..."

Nellie expelled a deep breath as the normalcy of day-to-day living ensued around her, serving to calm her down. She was safe—for now. Her badge made it so she was safe in the atrium, her protected status clear to one and all.

If she thought it odd that the huge man with the intense steel eyes hadn't followed her into the atrium, that he apparently didn't want others to see him, she dismissed the peculiarity of the situation as she threaded her way through the crowd and walked quickly toward the airbus railway.

She sighed, her head shaking slightly. She really needed a vacation.

Chapter 3

"Mother?" she whispered.

Her teeth sank down into her bottom lip as she slowly backed away from the beautiful red-haired woman who lay naked on the bed, her entire body convulsing. A man stood at the foot of the bed smiling down at his victim, a dirty syringe-like mechanism in his hand, pleased with what he'd done.

Nellie's eyes filled with tears as she clutched her Daffy-dolly to her chest. Her mother began frothing at the mouth, her perfect body violently shuddering. "Mommy no! Please!"

The intruder was startled. His dark head shot up, and then twisted around.

Daffy-dolly fell to the ground, forgotten.

"Daddy?" Nellie whispered.

Nellie gasped as she bolted upright in bed, sweat plastering rogue waves of hair to her forehead. She panted heavily as she slowly assimilated the fact that she'd been dreaming.

Just a dream.

This time.

Sucking in a large tug of air, she threaded her fingers through her hair, grabbing handfuls by the root, and fell backward into the extravagant silk pillow-bed. She closed her eyes and expelled the breath slowly.

"End it, Nellie," she whispered. "You're the only one who can end it."

* * * * *

He gasped as his small frame hit the ground with a thud, the impact knocking the breath from him. Unable to move, his body still stunned by the blow, he could only lay there in defenseless horror as a low growling sound drew closer.

His head came up slowly, and his eyes filled with tears, as they clashed with a blood-red gaze.

"Please mommy," he whispered. "Please don't hurt me."

She stilled, her razor-sharp black claws retreating a bit. He saw the awareness come back into her eyes, knew the precise moment when she realized she'd just tried to murder her own son...

"Help me!" she cried, scratching at her own face with her retreating claws. Her eyes, gray again, looked frantic, desperate. "If there is a god," she sobbed, "I beg of you to help me!"

He backed away as his mother began to convulse, afraid she would turn again. He was young, but he'd seen enough infected humans to understand that one day soon his mother would be lost to him for good…

And she'd never again come back.

Kerick bolted upright within the concealed cave, sweat plastering rogue waves of hair to his forehead. He panted heavily as he slowly assimilated the fact that he'd been dreaming.

Just a dream.

This time.

Sucking in a large tug of air, he threaded his fingers through his hair, grabbing handfuls by the root, and fell backward onto the cold slab of stone and warm animal hides. He closed his eyes and expelled the breath slowly.

"End it, Riley," he whispered. "You're the only one who can end it."

Chapter 4

This breaking news just in from the Hierarchy Security Command Centre:

Three Death Row inmates escaped from the Kong Penal Colony earlier this week, marking the first time in the history of Correctional Sector 12's existence that the maximum-security fortress was breached. The inmates left a gory trail of death in their wake, killing the warden and severely injuring five guards in the process of escaping...

Freshly showered, Nellie stood within the dwelling chamber of her domicile, readying herself for a grueling workday before indulging in breakfast. Her gaze flicked up to the virtual wall console. She absently watched the news story unfold as she twisted her long hair into a tight bun atop her head.

It is believed by the Hierarchy that the inmates have fled to the Dublin biosphere, where at least one of them was born and still holds strong Underground ties. The Altun Ha Hierarchy Command Centre has issued an official warning to the leaders of Biosphere 5, declaring the escapees armed and extremely dangerous.

She lost interest, not all that curious about news that was so far removed from her everyday life. Besides, she had a hell of a lot of work to finish today before the Fathom System's soiree tonight, she thought on a sigh.

Finished securing her hair into a neat bun, she strode toward the wall console, intent on turning it off as the first inmate's ebony face filled the virtual display screen.

All three escaped prisoners are known enemies of federated Earth: Elijah "The Slayer" Carter, shown here after his conviction in the grisly murder of Hierarchy leader Maxim Malifé in 2238, Xavier "Romeo" O'Connor, convicted in 2239 on several accounts of rape against three wives of Hierarchy leaders, and finally, the infamous "Grim Reaper", who was convicted in 2234 and sentenced to die for the brutal murders of no less than five Hierarchy leaders in biospheres as far reaching as Dublin and Prague. The "Grim Reaper", also known as Ker—

Rushed for time, Nellie flicked off the wall console. She padded into the auto-kitchen, found and peeled a banana, crammed a huge bite of the sweet fruit into her mouth, and schlepped toward the office in her domicile with Dr. Riley's journal in hand.

She sighed. She had a hell of a lot of work to do.

* * * * *

AND ALWAYS, NIGHT AND DAY, HE WAS IN THE MOUNTAINS AND IN THE TOMBS, CRYING, AND CUTTING HIMSELF WITH STONES...

Nellie ran a frustrated hand through her hair as she attempted for the thousandth plus time to figure out why Margaret Riley, an avowed atheist, had referenced ancient Biblical passages within her worn diary. If the scientist had done so, there had been a reason. She just had to figure out what precisely that reason was.

"The airbus shuttle to the Fathom Systems party leaves in forty-five minutes," her personal droid chimed out in a monotone. "I have laid out your body décor and it awaits you in your sleeping chamber."

Nellie's dark red head bobbed up into the droid's line of vision. Her eyes flicked over its silver body, the appearance of the expensive piece of machinery resembling that of a naked woman with skin made of steel. The only part of the droid that could pass for human was her pussy. It looked, felt, and carried the scent of a real female vagina. In a world where women were rare and men sought pleasure wherever they could get it, she was hardly surprised that droids had been modeled in such a fashion. "Thank-you, Cyrus 12."

The droid nodded, a perfect human affectation. "I will await you in your sleeping chamber, Dr. Kan."

That quickly Cyrus 12 was forgotten. Nellie buried her face back into the journal, the next entry catching her attention.

AND JESUS SAID UNTO HIM, COME OUT OF THE MAN, THOU UNCLEAN SPIRIT.

AND HE ASKED HIM, WHAT IS THY NAME? AND THE DEMON ANSWERED, SAYING, MY NAME IS LEGION, FOR WE ARE MANY.

"What are you trying to tell me, Dr. Riley?" Nellie murmured. She sighed, the diary dropping into her lap.

"Whatever it is, I'll figure it out," she promised, her hand running over the faded leather. "Just give me time," she whispered.

* * * * *

Twenty minutes later, Nellie stood in front of the image map in her bathing chamber, which presented to her how she looked in her body décor from all possible angles. She supposed she was pretty enough, but then again all females were. Scientists routinely engineered plainness in female fetuses out while the babies were still in vitro.

Her lips turned down into a frown when she considered the fact that the same engineering was never done on male fetuses. It was as common, if not more common, to see an unattractive man as it was to see a handsome one.

But women—women were a different story. Women were *always* a different story, she sighed. Even for something as simple as a corporate dinner party, like the one she would be attending tonight, Nellie was expected to show up half naked, while the male scientists in attendance would be permitted to wear any body décor of their choosing.

Her eyes flicked over the image map as she studied the body she'd been born into. Much of it had been engineered in the womb to one day give the man who purchased her as a wife the most pleasure possible, but some of it, like the color of her hair, was authentically her own. Geneticists were able to do many things, but they'd never figured out how to change the hair, skin, and eye color of fetuses—and have it stick. The colors always bounced back within the fifth year of life, proudly proclaiming themselves to be there.

And there was one other thing geneticists could no longer do, Nellie considered. They could no longer interfere with the gender of a human embryo.

When it had first become apparent that the females of the race were dying out, the male scientists had tried in desperation to stop any more would-be-mothers from breeding sons. But by then it had been too late, for the female reproduction system had evolved with its environment, rejecting embryos lacking a y chromosome, and for a solid thirty years not even one female birth had occurred. The three decades long famine of female offspring had transpired over eighty years ago, but the effect had turned out to be a profound and long-lasting one.

Nellie half-snorted as she thought back on a journal entry she'd read a few months ago in Margaret Riley's diary:

MEN. FOR THE MOST PART THEY ARE STUPID, PATHETIC CREATURES. JUST WHAT DID THOSE SCIENTISTS THINK WOULD HAPPEN TO THE NATURAL ORDER OF LIFE WHEN THEY DECIDED TO BEHAVE IN THE ROLE OF GODS? GOOD CYRUS, BUT MY FIVE YEAR OLD SON SHOWS MORE INTELLIGENCE THAN THEY EVER DID AT FORTY AND FIVE!

Nellie grinned at the memory. She slipped into her skirt as she absently glanced at the image map.

BIOLOGICALLY SPEAKING, THE MALE IS LESS VALUABLE THAN THE FEMALE. I SAY THIS NOT OUT OF FANATICISM, AS MANY IF NOT ALL OF MY COLLEAGUES PERPETUALLY ACCUSE ME OF, BUT OUT OF TRUTH.

THINK ABOUT IT: IF YOU HAVE A THOUSAND MEN AND ONE WOMAN, ALL THOUSAND OF THOSE MALES CAN FUCK THAT ONE WOMAN UNTIL THEIR COCKS DRY UP AND THEIR BALLS QUIT MAKING SEED, AND YET WHAT IS THE RESULT IN NINE MONTHS TIME? THE RESULT IS ONE, OR IN EXTREME CASES TWO TO THREE, BABES.

NOW PUT ONE MALE IN A ROOM OF A THOUSAND WOMEN, SPILLING HIS SEED LEFT AND RIGHT, AND WHAT IS THE RESULT IN NINE MONTHS TIME? A THOUSAND BABES OR MORE.

AS I SAID, THE MALE IS BIOLOGICALLY MORE EXPENDABLE THAN THE FEMALE...

Nellie studied her body intently on the image map, her eyes flicking over her form. She had been engineered in the womb like all other females had been so that when she grew into womanhood she would be the walking, talking, breathing epitome of male aesthetic pleasure.

Her legs were long and lithe, with just a hint of padding around the thighs to make it comfortable for the male to ride her body for long periods of time. Her breasts were huge—veritable melons—firm and perky, yet lush and soft. Her areolas were large, round, and rosy, and her nipples were generally stiff.

Her face had been hand-sculpted by a genetics artist in the image of male-perceived female perfection. Full lips, cat-like eyes, a small slip of a nose that pointed a tad upward at the tip…

But the dark red hair was hers, inherited from her mother. The creamy tanned coloring was also hers, the combined genetic result of her mother's pearly white skin and her father's darkly tanned one. The green eyes she'd inherited from her father, which probably explained why she avoided looking into them while gazing at the image map.

Nellie's gaze flicked down to the body décor she was wearing. She frowned.

The male scientists at tonight's soiree would be fully attired, but the only body décor Nellie had been permitted to don was a pair of sparkling gold high heeled boots, a heavy gold chain with the Fathom Systems emblem dangling from her hips that declared her protected, and a tight white skirt that started at the ankles and inched all the way up to just underneath her breasts so that it lifted them up to make them appear even bigger and more swollen than usual.

Her breasts, of course, were to be left non-attired.

Chapter 5

He refused to be defeated by a damned female. Dr. Nellie Kan should be naked and in chains, preparing herself to be auctioned off to a husband. She should not be in *his* lab, or rather, she should not be in the lab that would have been his had he gotten that promotion instead of Nellie.

Dr. Boris Karli motioned to the male graduate student he'd taken with him on safari to follow his lead. He knew that young Miklos was frightened, terrified even, but then so was Boris.

Nobody, not even the right-hand hired arms of the Hierarchy leaders themselves, ever dared to venture to the Outside. Life outside of the biospheres was violent and ruthless, for the only sorts that dwelled within the jungles were outlaws and sub-humans. The first group would cut your throat without hesitation that they might dig the yen chip out of your brain and steal your assets, while the second group would cut your throat with nary a qualm that they might dine upon you at their leisure.

No—the Outside was no place any man ever wanted to go. But then this was an extreme circumstance, he doggedly reminded himself.

"I-I don't know about this, Dr. Karli," Miklos whispered in a thick Russian accent. A hybrid insect, which had the body of a beetle and the small but sharp talons of a predator buzzed over his head, causing him to gulp. If that thing stung him, he'd be dead in an hour. "Nyet," he breathed out in Russian. "No, I will go no further. We are barely twenty yards outside the perimeter of the Altun Ha biosphere and already—"

"Silence!" Boris whispered back in an irritated voice. "Do you wish for Nellie Kan to develop a serum before we do?"

Miklos shrugged, not particularly caring. He doubted Dr. Karli would give him any credit for his help anyway. He knew he'd end up doing all the work in terms of developing the serum, the basis of which had been stolen from Dr. Kan's notes to begin with, and then Dr. Karli would act as though he had done it all himself and give neither Nellie nor Miklos any credit. "What is important is that a serum be developed, Doctor. It is not important who actually develops it."

Boris rolled his eyes and laughed without humor. "It sounds to me as though you've been sneaking some of Old Man Henders' virtual memory chips again, boy." He laughed harder when Miklos' face burned red. "I don't blame you for wanting to see the bitch in all her naked glory stroking that cunt of hers, but that hardly means she is a good scientist."

Actually, Miklos thought to himself, she was probably the most intelligent scientist he had met since he'd become a protégée. And the only scientist he'd met who actually seemed more interested in helping her fellow humans rather than seizing glory for her own reward. But Miklos could see for himself that Dr. Karli was already angry, so he kept his thoughts to himself.

"We are *males*," Boris spat out, his teeth gritting. "Males whose rightful positions in life have been usurped by a mindless, dimwitted female whose greatest asset is her huge tits." His jaw clenched unforgivingly. "Now cease your prattle and do as you're told."

Miklos' nostrils flared. Enough was enough. He was not about to surrender his life to the Outside in the name of Boris Karli and his misplaced loathing of Dr. Kan. "I am returning to the biosphere," he said simply, but firmly.

Dr. Karli shook an enraged finger at him. "You will never," he hissed, "work in my lab or at Fathom Systems again."

Miklos shrugged. "I doubt you hold such a power as to have me removed from Fathom Systems, but if you do then so be it. Losing my position in life is much more desirable than losing my life altogether." He grinned when Boris' cheeks went up in angry flames for they both knew he held no true clout within the Hierarchy. "Perhaps I shall ask Dr. Kan if she desires a male protégée," he taunted. His blue eyes twinkled as he mockingly saluted the doctor, and then turned on his heel to leave the jungle. He felt better than he had since the day he'd first arrived at Fathom Systems. "I bid you good day, Doctor."

Boris' eyes narrowed at the protégée's retreating back. His hand shook with rage as he balled it into a tight fist. If he had to go into the jungle alone, then so be it. To those with guts went the glory.

He realized, of course, that he only had one real shot at usurping Nellie's place in Fathom System's good graces, and that shot depended upon his developing a serum before the bitch did. How else could he hope to compete against her? he thought. The slut was always taking off her clothes, giving Henders his own little perverted jack-off material.

Unfortunately, the dimwitted little idiot had apparently figured out that her notes had been rifled through, for she'd locked them up in a keystroke sequence he hadn't been able to decode. But it didn't matter. He was Boris Karli—a *male*—and he would develop that damned serum before Nellie did if it was the last thing he ever accomplished.

Boris tightened his hold on the flash-stick, his senses on full alert. He ignored the frightening buzzing sounds of the hybrid insects hovering overhead and made his way deeper into the jungle.

He would find a nest of sub-humans. He would abstract a bit of DNA from them, and then he would develop that serum.

To those with guts went the glory.

Chapter 6

Nellie stood at the far end of the massive ballroom within the Fathom Systems corridor of the Altun Ha biosphere and stared unblinkingly at a star-carrier cruising by in the nighttime sky. As she stared out of the black glass, which was actually a misnomer for the "glass" was made of mass-produced black diamonds from a planet in a neighboring galaxy, she absently wondered where the star-carrier was headed to.

Perhaps the planet Kalast, she thought dreamily, her index finger swirling around the rim of the chalice of spirits she held. She'd always wanted to see Kalast, but had never had the opportunity. The planet was allegedly red-tinted and filled with lush mountainscapes…sort of like a habitable Mars. And, even better, Kalast was an oasis for females as the government was operated solely by women.

Nellie sighed, realizing as she did that there was no use in wishing to ever lay eyes on Kalast. Female Earthlings were forbidden by the Federation Charter of 2195 to venture off-planet without a male escort. And even then they had to be bound to him with sensory chains. No male would be fool enough to vacation on a planet where his woman would have an opportunity to flee from him without the security of sensory chains. The typical male Earthling had to save his yen for many, many years in order to purchase a wife; he certainly wouldn't chance losing one after paying such a steep price to own her.

"Dr. Kan, what a pleasure it is to see you again."

Nellie heard the familiar voice greet her at the precise moment she felt two large male hands wrap around her from behind and palm her non-attired breasts. She thought nothing of it when he began stroking her nipples, for it was the legal right of a male to caress an unmarried female in any way he chose to do so, so long as she was lower in the Hierarchy than he. She smiled, then turned on her boot heel to greet her former professor and mentor. She handed her chalice over to a passing by droid. "Dr. Lorin, I didn't expect to see you here tonight."

He smiled, his Cajun inherited brown eyes crinkling at the corners. "Good Cyrus, but it's been a long time, Nellie." He slowly ran two tanned hands over her swollen breasts, then began to softly massage her stiff nipples with the pads of his thumbs while he engaged her in conversation. "I don't believe we've had the delight of attending the same corporate party since you were under my tutelage."

"C'est vrai," she agreed in the native French tongue of his homeland biosphere. *That's true.*

Treymor Lorin had to be in his late fifties by now, yet he was still as handsome and distinguished looking as ever, if not more so, she thought. Nellie had always been grateful that when she'd taken the chance and petitioned to the Hierarchy for the right to forgo the marriage auction block in lieu of a career, it had been to a man as handsome and sophisticated as Dr. Lorin that she had been given.

She could have ended up anywhere and been given to anyone of the Hierarchy's choosing, but she had been fortunate that she'd been placed under the protection of a respectable man like the esteemed professor. Treymor Lorin was everything her current protector Vorice Henders was not—honorable, dedicated to his work, and loyal to those under his protection.

Nellie reflected on the five years she'd lived with and learned from Dr. Lorin as he proceeded to bring her up to date on all the new changes in his life and work. Apparently he now had another female protégée living with him, a young woman whom the Hierarchy had placed with him a few months back. She was pleased by such knowledge, and even more delighted to hear that the young female planned to gain employment at Fathom Systems when her years of tutelage were over, for it had long been Nellie's contention that the mega-conglomerate company needed more female scientists within its ranks.

"Is she taking to her studies well?" Nellie asked. Her eyes closed briefly when the beginnings of arousal stirred in her belly from the gentle nipple massage Dr. Lorin was giving to her.

He grinned, his thumbs working her stiff nipples into a pleasurous ache. "She's flourishing more quickly than the hybrid peoples of planet Rolfi can procreate."

She chuckled at that. "She must be quite intelligent then."

His look was thoughtful. "In most subjects, yes, but she's having a Kong of a time getting the gist of virtual display theory."

One dark red eyebrow shot up. "Good Cyrus, I seem to recall having trouble with that very subject once myself! But look at me now," she encouraged, "I know everything there is to know about it." She nodded definitively. "Your new protégée will learn, Dr. Lorin, I've no doubt."

He cocked his head, his eyes wandering over her face. He deepened the nipple massage as he studied her features, his fingers expertly remembering how she liked it best. "She reminds me of you," he admitted, "in that she enjoys having her beautiful breasts laved with attention." He grinned. "Though I daresay it's an activity I never minded indulging you in."

Highly aroused, Nellie stared at him through hooded eyes. "She's a lucky protégée," she murmured, trying to keep her thoughts on the topic at hand. But Dr. Lorin was correct when he'd stated that she enjoyed having her breasts massaged, so keeping her thoughts linear to the discussion was proving difficult.

Her former protector backed her up against the black glass wall, and then pressed his erection against her tummy. When he released her breasts in favor of grabbing at her skirt and hoisting it up to her waist, she felt a moment's shyness at having her intimate triangle of dark red curls exposed to the ever-greedy gaze of all the males in the ballroom.

And yet conversely she knew that there was no point in being shy, for it would be considered tactless and rude to refuse to satiate the lust of a former protector while she still had no permanent master. It was implicitly understood by all in attendance that should Dr. Lorin decide to fuck her right here and now for all to see, Nellie was expected to not only submit to his desire, but to show gratitude for the privilege of being wanted by a male so esteemed.

At eighteen, when Nellie had first been sent to Dr. Lorin's domicile, she had felt very grateful for the older man's protection and instruction. He had schooled her in all things scientific, and in exchange she had handed over to him the use of her body as it is required of a female protégée to do.

Dr. Lorin had never balked at the opportunity, but had reveled in it instead. He had been in his late forties and she just eighteen when she'd been sent to live with him, and he had delighted in her youth. She could still recall the way he had gritted his teeth every time he'd sank his cock into her young, tight pussy.

She could still remember lots of things — like how he'd always commanded her to sit on his lap and spread her thighs on the days when her grueling schoolwork had required lectures. The entire time he'd lectured her his fingers had played with her pussy, sometimes rubbing her clit, and sometimes merely contenting themselves with running through her soft nether hair. And inevitably when the day's lesson was finished, he would bend her over the desk and thrust into her from behind, pounding into her until he found completion.

At eighteen she hadn't minded turning over the use of her body to her protector, for she had understood it was his right as her temporary master to reap the benefits of having a rare human female under his tutelage. And yet as she stood here in the ballroom and felt him press his erection against her bared mons, she found that at thirty-two she did mind. She was no longer dwelling in his domicile and didn't feel as though she owed him reparation any longer. Indeed, she had given him all the sex he'd desired back when it had been required by the law for her to do so.

Dr. Lorin backed up slightly and replaced his erection with his hand. Nellie felt his gossamer white robe tickle her thigh when he took a step back. She immediately relaxed when he began running his fingers through her triangle, for she realized he wasn't about to fuck her in front of the entire chamber. If all he meant to do was stroke her into orgasm, well, that much she could deal with.

"I've missed your kitty-cat," Dr. Lorin said thickly as his fingers leisurely combed through the soft curls.

Nellie blushed, having forgotten that's what he'd always referred to her pussy as back when he'd been her protector. She hadn't minded him calling it a kitty-cat when she'd been eighteen, but again, she found that at thirty-two she did mind. She wasn't a child any longer. She was a woman—and a scientist.

Naïve girl protégées had kitty-cats. Mature women scientists had pussies.

Her breath caught in the back of her throat when his index and middle fingers began rubbing her clit in a slow, circular motion. She moaned softly when the fingers of his other hand came back up to play with her nipples.

"Such a succulent cunt you have, Nellie," he murmured. "So wet and sweet, and so swollen."

She closed her eyes on a whimper, her body responding to his words and his touch. It had been so long since she'd been with a man—far too long.

"And these nipples…" he praised her, his hand running worshipfully over both breasts. He clucked his tongue. "I've never seen nipples quite this color before, Nellie. But then you already know that, chere."

She did know that. Dr. Lorin had always been quite taken with her nipples. Her aureoles were large and round, and a tad puffy. Her nipples were long and stiff, and colored a deep, rare rouge. Their coloring was so unique, in fact, that she knew her price on the auction block would be steep if ever she decided to allow such an event as marriage to transpire. It was the same with her hair. The rare dark red coloring of the pelt of curls between her thighs was highly sought after on auction blocks world over.

Nellie expelled a breathy moan as her former mentor toyed with her nipples and clit. Her eyes still closed, she tilted her head back and rested it on the black glass wall as her orgasm drew rapidly near. The sound of boisterous conversations ensuing around her was drowned out by the fast beat of her heart. The reverberations from the techno-opera musique the band was playing faded into the dim recesses of her mind.

Clearly, it had been far too long since a male had brought her to peak. She could think of nothing but the need for completion, the need for—

The hair at the nape of her neck began to stir, much as it had last evening in the lab when the ventilation system had been purposely shut off. That eerie sensation was back again, that feeling of being watched. Watched and…intensely coveted.

Nellie's cat-like green eyes flew open. As if she knew precisely where to look, as if it didn't matter that the party chamber she was standing in was three balconies high and a thousand feet across, her head came up slowly, her line of vision immediately honing in on the second balcony balustrade.

She sucked in her breath.

The man—*him*.

The giant looked much the same tonight as he had yesterday when she'd bumped into him in the corridor. He wore the same hooded black robe, the same grim features, and those eyes...

Those intense steel gray eyes never strayed from her the entire time Dr. Lorin continued to stroke her toward orgasm. She knew the man could see everything there was to see about her, for there was no body décor concealing her breasts and her skirt had been hoisted up to her waist.

Nellie's eyes clashed with the giant's and a chill of foreboding passed through her. He was angry — very angry — and somehow, though she didn't understand how she knew it, she realized that the man was angry with Dr. Lorin for touching her. And possibly with her as well.

The man's eyes strayed from her face and down to her breasts. He studied them intently, causing her already stiff nipples to unwittingly pucker further. She felt hands grab her breasts and pinch appreciatively at her nipples and it was only then that she realized Dr. Lorin had invited his colleagues over to help him make her come. But she couldn't concentrate on them. She could only stare up at the balcony...

The giant's nostrils flared as his eyes strayed down further, to the triangle of dark red curls. He gazed at her pussy so intensely, so possessively, that Nellie half-wondered if he'd managed to brand it without an auctioneer's branding tool to aid him.

"Such a lovely kitty-cat, Nellie," Dr. Lorin praised. "I want her to purr for me."

Another male laughed at that. "Losing your golden touch, Treymor?"

"Indeed," a third male chimed in as he pinched at one nipple, "she's yet to purr, Trey."

Her former protector grunted at the challenge. "I shall remedy that oversight immediately."

Nellie felt inexplicable panic bubble up inside of her as the trio of esteemed males stripped her of all body décor and carried her to a black glass table located right below the giant. He was only one balcony up from her and the three scientists had splayed her out before him, unknowingly giving him a private show.

She felt one pair of male lips latch around a plump nipple, and then a second pair latched around her other one. The males sucked on them like treats, bringing to mind boys tasting lollipops for the first time. When Dr. Lorin settled himself on a chair between her spread legs and began lapping at her pussy, her gaze flew up to the giant's.

Nellie's eyes widened at his look of promised retribution to come. Whether that retribution was to be dealt out to her, or to the males touching and kissing on her, she couldn't say. But the huge man's clenched jaw and flaring nostrils said it all: he thought that he owned her, believed that her former protector had no right to taste a cunt he clearly considered to belong to him.

She blinked at the incredulity of her thoughts, for they made no sense. She didn't know the giant, had never seen him before yesterday, so how on Earth could he possibly be feeling the emotions she was pinning on him?

"Purr for me," she heard Dr. Lorin growl against her clit.

Nellie gasped as her former protector thrust his tongue into her pussy, then groaned when he slurped her clit into his mouth and suckled it vigorously.

The male scientists licking and sucking her nipples increased the pressure of their mouths, driving her wild. She expelled a worried breath as her gaze flew back up to the balcony, realizing as she did that orgasm was inevitable. It was madness, of course, to worry over what the grim-looking stranger might do to punish her, but the feeling was still there.

Nellie's head fell back on a gasp and her eyes closed. She wanted to stop herself from coming, but—

"*Ooooh.*" She burst on a low moan, her splayed legs trembling from the violence of it.

She felt her nipples stab upwards into the still suckling mouths of the males latched onto her there, and could hear Dr. Lorin's appreciative *mmmm* sounds as he lapped up all her pussy juice.

Her huge breasts heaved up and down from under the males' mouths, perspiration dotting her cleavage as she came down from the sensual high. Her senses coming back to her, and her memory along with it, her eyes flew open and up to the balcony.

Gone—the man was gone.

Nellie blinked, wondering if she hadn't imagined him to begin with. There was no way he could have gotten off the balcony without descending the staircase and that would have taken some time to do. More time than she'd had her eyes shut for at any rate.

Five minutes later, Nellie closed her eyes and sighed when it appeared that the males sucking on her nipples had no intention of letting them go any time soon. She knew human females were scarce, so this was no doubt a true treat for them. They brought to mind the image of suctioning fish whose mouths had latched around a lure and couldn't let go.

From between her splayed thighs she heard Dr. Lorin chuckling at his colleagues' infatuation with her breasts. As he ran his fingers through her drenched nether hair, she idly listened while he beckoned a young male of eighteen over to look at her puffed up pussy. She could tell from the sound of the boy's labored breathing that he'd never been this close to a real cunt before, had probably only seen them in virtual reality movies and four-dimensional magazines.

Nellie took a deep breath and expelled it. She really needed a vacation.

Chapter 7

December 21, 2249 A.D.

And I stood upon the sand of the sea, and saw a beast rise up out of the sea...And they worshipped the beast, saying, Who is like unto the beast? Who is able to make war with him?

And he causeth all, both small and great, rich and poor, free and bond, to receive a mark in their right hand, or in their foreheads: And that no man might buy or sell, save he that had the mark...

Here is wisdom. Let him that hath understanding count the number of the beast for it is the number of a man; and his number is six hundred, threescore, and six.

Wide-eyed, Nellie gently set the journal down on the desk she kept within her domicile. Her gaze flicked back to the last entry she'd read, a passage from the Book of

Revelation that had been painstakingly scrawled out in Margaret Riley's hand.

HERE IS WISDOM. LET HIM THAT HATH UNDERSTANDING COUNT THE NUMBER OF THE BEAST FOR IT IS THE NUMBER OF A MAN; AND HIS NUMBER IS SIX HUNDRED, THREESCORE, AND SIX.

Nellie slowly rose to her feet. Pale as the moon, she turned on her heel and padded out of her office and into her bathing chamber. She stopped when she reached it, coming to a halt in front of the four-dimensional image map.

Staring unblinkingly at her image from all angles, she raised a trembling hand to her skull and ran a single finger over her chip-implanted forehead. The chip made it so she could buy and sell, so she could live within any biosphere of federated Earth...

She swallowed roughly. The chip had been manufactured by Fathom Systems. It had been the company's pet project for over fifty years until it had finally been perfected twenty and some odd years ago.

Nellie closed her eyes briefly, then opened them again and stared at the image map. In that moment she became chillingly aware of the fact that her life would never be the same again. What had started out as a quest to ease the suffering of sub-humans had grown into a search for a truth she couldn't even begin to comprehend. And, she feared, if she was successful, if she ever found out just what that truth was, it would probably get her killed. Or infected. Or…worse.

She bit down onto her bottom lip as her finger tracked the area where she knew the chip to be located behind the skin of her forehead. She stilled, her finger abruptly coming to a halt.

The chip, she uneasily considered, had a name. Officially termed the *Biological Enzyme And Skin-cell Tracker*, or simply the *BEAST* for short, it had taken the fusion of six natural gases, six strategically extrapolated brain cells, and six molecules of a liquid substance indigenous to planet Kalast known as Erodium to create a chip that could be hosted within the human body without dire consequences.

Six gases, six molecules, six brain cells…

666.

Nellie took a deep breath and expelled it. Why the Kong hadn't she taken that vacation?

* * * * *

An hour and three chalices of spirits later, Nellie sank down onto her lush pillow-bed feeling overwhelmed. She was also feeling drunk, and decided she might just stay that way.

Like the ill-fated heroine in a dramatically tragic virtual reality movie, her hand flew to her forehead and her eyes closed on a martyr's sigh. All she needed was for the famous and studly cyber-droid Cabel Modem to whisk into her domicile and steal her away to help him on a secret mission in galaxies hitherto unknown and the tragic heroine imagery would be complete.

She sighed, deciding that a fourth chalice of spirits could hardly do much damage to her already inebriated state. In fact, the world might seem a much better place a hallucination or two later.

Frowning, she stood up and padded out of the sleeping chamber and into the auto-kitchen. "Cyrus 12," she grumbled, "have you fixed the slave yet?"

Slave was the generic term for a machine hooked up within the kitchens of most domiciles. Slaves made it so all free citizens could receive any buyable item available in their sector with a mere verbal command stating what it was that they wanted. Body décor, spirits, hot meals—so long as you knew what you wanted, and so long as your chip had enough yen in its memory bank, the slave could fetch your heart's desire for you within seconds.

"Affirmative, Dr. Kan," the droid said in a monotone, "but it will take an hour or so before it's been recharged and has reached online status."

Nellie sighed. She'd gone and drank the last bit of spirits she'd had left about ten minutes ago. What a damned day. "Thanks anyway, Cyrus 12. I suppose I'll retire to my sleeping chamber."

"Do you require me to deactivate for the remainder of the evening, Dr. Kan?"

She shrugged her shoulders dismissively. Turning to walk back to her pillow-bed, she stepped out of her lab coat to get naked for sleeping. "Yes, go ahead and recharge, Cyrus 12." She could do without the droid's protection for a few scant hours. Besides, her domicile possessed all of Fathom System's latest and greatest security technology. She doubted even a god could breach the fortress should one be so inclined as to try. "I'm going to bed."

Chapter 8

Boris Karli cried out in pain as he stumbled toward the entrance to the cave he'd found. The bite dealt to him by the mutated insect was deep and required immediate attention. If he didn't shoot himself up with a drug that could counteract the poison immediately, he'd be dead outside of an hour.

In the throes of agony, he gritted his teeth against the pain as he fell to his knees at the mouth of the cave, unable to walk.

I need to be in some manner of shelter, he thought hysterically, the fear of impending death at last swamping him.

Using what little strength he had left, he came up on all fours and crawled into the cave, determined to get inside before he shot himself up. The pain of crawling was so intense, so sharp and shooting, he was unable to restrain himself from gasping at the agony of it.

But finally, as he'd known in all of his arrogance that he would, he made it inside the dimly lit cavern and scooted up against a wall. His hands violently shaking, he dropped his satchel to the earthen ground and fumbled through its contents until he located the proper syringe.

"You can do this, Karli," he ground out, perspiration soaking him. His hand trembling, he palmed the syringe, snatched it out of the medical satchel, and buried it deeply into his arm. He cried out as the drug lanced through him like fire, the feeling akin to acid shooting through his veins.

A minute later, when the pain began to subside and his heart rate began its descent to homeostasis, he chuckled aloud, pleased with himself. Nellie Kan might have a cunt and huge tits, but she was no Boris Karli. Information that had taken the bitch years to collect would all be his in the matter of days. As soon as he located a nest of sub-humans and gathered some DNA samples to take back to the lab, he would be able to develop a serum in the matter of a week or less.

And then, he thought arrogantly, Nellie Kan would cease to matter at Fathom Systems. A fait accompli.

A blood-chilling scream echoed throughout the cave, sending goosebumps down Boris' spine. His eyes wide, he swallowed nervously as he quietly stood up and tightened his hold on the flash-stick. A low, tortured moan followed by another scream pierced the air, causing the scientist to tremble.

If he was right, an outlaw had just been attacked by a sub-human. That meant to Boris that the sub-human's attention would be snagged by the dying carcass it was dining on, allowing him precious time to immobilize it.

He took a shaky breath and expelled it, then fumbled through his satchel for a vial of numbing spray. The spray would render the sub-human immobile long enough for him to collect a DNA sample, after which time Boris would simply kill the creature with the flash-stick.

Creeping slowly into the bowels of the cave, Boris made his way toward the innermost chamber of the cavern — the sub-human sanctuary where he heard the sounds coming from. As he drew nearer, the horrific noises grew more intense, inducing his stomach muscles to knot.

You must do this, Boris, he mentally reiterated. He swiped at his dripping brow with a forearm. *To those with guts go the glory…*

His body began to shake uncontrollably as he approached the inner chamber, knowing as he did that when he rounded the corner he would be faced with a nest of sub-humans. He had no idea how many of them there would be, or how hungry they would still be, which was the most frightening aspect of his impending showdown with fate.

When he quietly crept into the cave's inner sanctuary, when he at last laid eyes on the species he had spent days tracking, he was so shocked by what he saw that the hand holding the flash-stick fell to his side, forgotten.

There was no outlaw in here being dined upon, he realized, his stomach churning. He gazed surrealistically at the scene before him, vomit creeping up his throat and threatening expulsion. "The species is breeding," he murmured.

The Hierarchy did not know that sub-humans could breed amongst themselves. If they had known, Boris told himself, they would have taken the threat imposed by the Outside a lot more seriously than they did.

Boris watched in horror as the new mother finished birthing the last of her three monsters. When it was done, when all three fanged babies had come out from between her legs, she gathered them together and walked them toward the other side of the cavern where a sub-human male, the babies' apparent father, had been haphazardly thrown, his legs broken, unable to run away.

The sub-human male screamed in terror, realizing his fate. The female predator, showing no pity or remorse, placed her hungry young beside the body of their father, then sat back and watched while their serrated teeth tore chunks from his flesh.

Boris closed his eyes and whimpered, the sounds of pain and terror the male was eliciting overwhelming to him. It was horrid and blood-curdling…a literal nightmare.

He supposed that from a scientific standpoint he shouldn't be surprised, for sub-human females weren't the only species of predators that killed off the male either during the act of copulation or immediately following the birth of her babes. The female preying mantis ripped off the head of its mate during the act of copulation in order to get pregnant. The female black widow spider spun a sticky web so her mate couldn't escape her clutches, allowing him to live until her eggs hatched, after which time she fed him to her young. Even a species of mega-raptors back in the age of dinosaurs had used the same method; after the female's eggs had hatched, she lunged down upon her mighty thighs, whipped up into the air and spun around, and gutted her mate with one deadly slice dealt from her massive talon, spilling his innards for her newborn young to dine upon.

Boris knew that the killing off of the male was common enough amongst predators. But knowing it and watching it were two different things. The male was dying slowly, agonizingly, unable to move, unable to defend himself.

Closing his eyes briefly and willing himself to calm down, he took a deep breath and told himself to get out of there. *Now.* While the female's attention was snagged and he still had a chance.

Boris turned on his heel and ran as fast as he could, his heart thumping madly against his chest, his feet kicking up dirt and pebbles as he fled for his life. He ran out of the inner sanctuary and headed straight for a steep incline that he knew would spit him back out into the jungle.

A low growl sounded from behind him, getting closer and then closer still. He willed his legs to move faster, a small cry of terror erupting from him. He would never make it, he realized. She was closing in on him. She would —

Boris expelled a breath of relief when he remembered the flash-stick. Halting in his tracks, his nostrils flared in renewed arrogance as he spun around on his heel and aimed the sites of the flash-stick where the creature should have been standing.

But wasn't.

He gasped when the flash-stick was snatched from his hands, and then cried out in pain when he was violently thrown to the ground in an act that snapped the bones in his legs like frail branches. His jaw agape, his gaze shot upward.

He screamed.

The female was hovering above him, her mouth forming a sickly smile that still showed the bloodstains of her last kill. Bits of flesh were wedged in between her serrated teeth, a grotesque reminder of what was in store for him.

Boris gasped. "Please," he muttered, his hands coming up in a futile effort to shield himself. "Sweet Cyrus, please do not!"

As he heard the hissing sound she made, as he saw a set of black claws lash out at his belly and spill his innards on the cavern floor, he heard the scampering of tiny feet come up quickly behind him.

His last thought before dying was that the children had apparently finished dining on their father.

And, he thought as he surrealistically watched the three tiny creatures slurp up his intestines, they were still hungry.

Chapter 9

Groggy with sleep, Nellie's forehead wrinkled in confusion when, from somewhere in the far corners of her mind, it occurred to her that her domicile security system had just emitted a low frequency buzzing sound. The noise was familiar, she thought sleepily, but she was so tired that she couldn't quite place from where—

Her eyes flew open. Her breathing stilled. Wide-eyed, and now very awake, she immediately realized precisely what that low frequency buzzing sound meant.

The sector's security system had been breached. And, more importantly to her peace of mind, her own domicile's security system had been compromised.

Her heart rate soaring, her breathing labored, Nellie bolted upright in the pillow-bed and scrambled to her feet. Her gaze flew wildly about the sleeping chamber as she tried to find some manner of weapon. Swallowing roughly, and growing more terrified by the second, she quietly inched her way towards the adjoining bathing chamber, her instincts screaming to get out now.

One step. Two steps. Three...

A dull thudding sound came from her domicile's auto-kitchen, confirming the fact that someone had just broken in. The intruder had somehow managed to crawl through the sector's ventilation system, for it was through the auto-kitchen that all domiciles were hooked up to the public air.

Nellie's eyes flicked toward the bathing chamber. If the intruder had just entered the auto-kitchen, she thought with a spark of hope, then she still had time to sneak out through the hidden panel behind her image map...

Turning abruptly, she bolted toward the bathing chamber, her breath coming in pants. When she reached the closed sliding doors, she frantically pressed a palm to the DNA scanner, biting down onto her lip as she waited for the doors to slide open with a whoosh.

They never did.

"Please," Nellie cried out softly, afraid for her life. She had no idea who had just broken into her domicile but given the fact that she'd been studying Margaret Riley's journal in secret she feared the worst—she feared it was a member of the Hierarchy who had managed to find out what she'd been up to and had thus come to silence her.

Throwing her palm back up against the DNA scanner, her body began to violently tremble with fear of impending death. Ice cold terror lanced through her, inducing her skin to goosebump and her nipples to harden as she broke out into a cold sweat. Sweet Cyrus, she thought, please don't let me die this way!

A whooshing sound filled the sleeping chamber a second later, only the noise hadn't come from the sliding doors of her bathing chamber. It had come from the other set of doors. The ones that led into the domicile proper. The ones, she thought on a soft cry, that someone would use to get to her if they'd just broken in through the auto-kitchen.

Nellie closed her eyes briefly as she placed her shaking palm one last time against the DNA scanner.

Nothing.

She laid her head against the doors, defeated. Her killer-to-be had managed to disengage the bathing chamber doors without disengaging the ones he needed to get to her.

Shaking, she lifted her head and slowly turned around, determined to face her executioner with dignity. She would not die a coward, she told herself with more staunch than she felt. She would look her murderer defiantly in the eye while—

"You can't escape, Nellie."

Her head flew up at the sound of the deep, rumbled voice. She squinted her eyes, trying in vain to make out the shape of the man who'd come to kill her. It was no use. Apparently the domicile's illumination system had been tampered with as well. All she could see was a large figure clad in what looked to be black.

"Just kill me and get it over with," she breathed out. Her breasts heaving, she backed up as far as she could against the bathing chamber doors.

"Now why would I want to do that?" the deep voice rumbled back. "After all the trouble I've gone through to have you for my own."

She knew he was getting closer to her. She couldn't see him, but she could hear him, feel him, smell him, sense him…

He took another step forward, and one half of his face was illuminated by a pale moonbeam.

A hooded black robe. A large, extremely muscular frame. Intense, steel gray eyes…

"Oh my god." Nellie's eyes widened when she realized who it was that had come to murder her. She should have figured out he'd been sent by the Hierarchy the day she'd first bumped into him. Only a hired assassin would be as big as this male; none but a hired assassin would have the occasion to acquire a musculature of that size.

She gasped when, in a lightning quick movement, the stranger's hand shot out and he wrapped a set of callused fingers around her neck. "Please," she whimpered, her earlier promise to herself to remain brave forgotten, "please make it quick and painless."

The callused hand worked its way downward, slowly running from her neck to her breasts. He used the palm of his hand to lightly graze the tips of her nipples, while his other hand found her pussy and threaded through the triangle there. "Painless—that's up to you," he murmured. "But quick…never."

Nellie gulped, wondering exactly what he'd meant by that enigmatic statement. Wondering too if they were talking about the same thing. "Who are you?" she whispered, her mind frantic. She wanted to cling to any shred of hope the giant might throw her way, wanted to believe he wasn't from the Hierarchy. But if he wasn't from the Hierarchy, what was it he wanted from her?

The feel of a long, thick erection poking against her belly caused Nellie's breathing to still. Her cat-green eyes widened in dawning comprehension. But—

No…

"Males don't chance imprisonment or worse just to illegally claim a woman," she shakily informed him, her breath coming out in a rush. Dismantling her security system would have required extinguishing the system throughout the entire sector. Such was madness. Sheer lunacy. He could have been caught at any stage of the game.

A callused finger stroked one of her nipples. His other hand remained at her pussy, playing in it. "All mine now," he murmured.

Her eyes rounded to the shape of full moons when it finally struck Nellie that the man had done just what she'd thought no man would ever be foolish enough, or bold enough, to do. As crazy as it sounded, as unbelievable as it was, the giant had brought the security system of an entire sector down to its knees just to fuck her. And, she thought on a nervous swallow, to own her.

Oh yes, she realized when his intense eyes hooded in lust, this male wanted more from her than a quick fuck. He meant to keep fucking her — he meant to master her.

The stranger was frighteningly cunning, yet she could practically see the direction his thoughts were going in as if they were being displayed before her in a virtual reality movie. He would simply make it look as though she'd left the perimeter of her protection, allowing him to claim her legally. Inferring that he had the right to take her, no male would interfere with his claim of ownership when he took the claim to the public arena.

And she would be at the mercy of a madman. Forever.

Terrified, trembling, and having no idea exactly what fate the stranger meant to relegate her to, Nellie opened her mouth to scream.

She'd barely dragged air into her lungs to make a sound when her cry for help was abruptly cut off by a rough palm slapping over her mouth.

Sweet Cyrus, she thought hysterically, please don't let him take me! If he took her away he could do anything to her and nobody would be the wiser. He could pass her around to friends that they all might share of her body, he could...good Cyrus, he could do anything. And worse yet, her peers would think she was dead. Unless, of course, he went public with his claim of ownership.

In the throes of a violent panic, Nellie used all of her strength to shove away from the huge stranger, but a quick pinch to her neck thwarted any effort she might have made to escape.

She blinked, then stumbled into his arms. A second later, the world went black.

Chapter 10

December 22, 2249 A.D.

Nellie made a soft moaning sound as she slowly came-to. She blinked a few times in rapid succession while her eyes adjusted to the dim lighting. When she could see again, when she was able to make heads or tails of her surroundings, she attempted to sit up, only to realize that she couldn't.

Her eyes widened when it dawned on her that she was chained up. A shackle on either wrist and a shackle on either ankle, her arms were chained above her head to an iron pike jutting out from the dirt wall behind her. Her feet had been chained in such a way that her legs were spread wide open and bent at the knee, completely exposing her pussy. A single animal fur had been draped over her, but she was otherwise totally nude.

She closed her eyes briefly, trying to figure a way out of her predicament. Perhaps if she—

She sighed. Who was she kidding? She'd been shackled with sensory chains. If she did escape, she would never do it and live to tell about it. She could only wander as far as the chains had been preprogrammed to allow her. For all she knew the giant might have instructed the chains to detonate within a foot of her lying position.

The sound of approaching voices caused Nellie's heart to beat rapidly. Not knowing what else to do, she abruptly closed her eyes and feigned unconsciousness when the voices entered the chamber she'd been placed in.

"Shh, we've got to be quiet."

There was a pause, and then, "I don't know about this, Kieran. If Kerick finds out he'll kill us."

Nellie could surmise from their voices that the males were young. Seventeen, maybe eighteen at best. Their next words confirmed it, for they were obviously too young to have enough yen to visit a Pussy Parlour.

"Don't you wanna see what a real cunt looks like?"

"Well yeah but—"

"All we're gonna do is look. That's all. Just a quick look and we'll leave. My brother will never know."

Another short pause. "What if the female wakes up? What if she tells him?"

Kieran sighed. "There's no way she'll wake up. She ain't been down here long enough."

That seemed to appease the other boy. "Okay then." His voice squeaked. "Let's do it."

Nellie could sense their growing excitement, could have sworn she'd heard both of them swallow in anticipation as they made their way across the chamber. When they reached the slab of stone and animal hides she'd been chained on, she felt one of the boys put his hand on the scrap of animal fur that had been draped over her body to give warmth.

His hand stilled. "Are you ready to see this, Alasdair?" Kieran murmured.

"Fuck yeah," Alasdair whispered back. "Take it off her, amigo."

A tug later, Nellie felt the animal fur fall from her body. Her nipples instantly stiffened from the chill in the air, and she experienced a tremor of arousal when a puff of cold wind hit her clit.

"Sweet Cyrus," Kieran said thickly. He traced her pussy lips with his index finger, rubbing all over the sleek folds of flesh. Nellie willed herself to feel no arousal, for what good it did. Still, she didn't want to give away the fact that she was awake to the curious teenage boys.

"What does it feel like?" Alasdair asked a bit hoarsely.

"Soft. And wet."

Alasdair gulped. "I want to feel it."

A second hand found her pussy. Fingers ran through her nether hair, then fell lower.

The first hand opened up her vaginal lips, stretching them.

"Look at this," Kieran whispered. A finger gently poked at her clit. "Shit, she's beautiful. Ripe as a berry."

"Looks even better than in the movies." The second hand left her pussy. "If you're gonna play with her cunt," Alasdair said quietly, "then I want to play with her tits for a while."

"Cyrus! They're big, ain't they?" Kieran thought things over for a second. "Okay, but let's trade places in five minutes, amigo. That way we both get to play with everything."

Nellie didn't know whether to laugh or cry when the teenagers began exploring her body in earnest. The arousal she experienced was made a thousand times more pronounced by the fact that she had to remain perfectly still lest she alert the boys to the fact that she was wide awake. No matter what they did, no matter how they touched her, she knew she had to will herself from coming.

For the next twenty minutes, Nellie was tortured in a way she'd never before thought of as painful. But then again, usually when her cunt and nipples were being poked and prodded, licked and sucked on, she was allowed release.

"You think you can talk your brother into letting us fuck her?" Alasdair's mouth unlatched from her erect nipple long enough to ask the question.

"I doubt it," Kieran grumbled.

And then Kieran did something Nellie had been praying the teenager wouldn't figure out to do. He lowered his face between her legs and greedily began sucking on her clit.

Beads of sweat broke out on her forehead.

"Mmmm, mmmm mmmmm," Kieran said dreamily from around her clit, half talking and half sucking on it, "she tastes so damn good."

Her stomach knotted. Desire shot hot and fast throughout her entire body.

"Her nipples are getting stiffer," Alasdair mumbled. He kissed the tip of one, then lowered his mouth to the other one and wrapped his lips around it.

Kieran's breathing grew increasingly labored. She could tell he wanted something from her, but was too unschooled to know exactly what. And then, his breathing frenzied, his face dove hard for her pussy and slurped up the clit. With a groan he sucked her hard, moaning against her cunt while he sucked, and sucked, and—

Nellie's body trembled violently inside as she burst. She didn't know how she managed it, would never know where the control came from, but she managed to keep from crying out, managed even to keep her breathing under control.

"Mmmmmm," Kieran said appreciatively. "If you suck on her cunt long enough it makes juice."

Alasdair's mouth unlatched from her stiff nipple with a popping sound. "No shit?" His head came up. "Lemme try."

Nellie mentally groaned when he did just that. For the next half hour she lay there, still as stone, while the boys repeatedly took turns sucking on her pussy until it made the juice they wanted to taste. They lapped it up like dogs, draining her over and over, again and again.

And then came the final bout. Kieran and Alasdair ate her out at the same time, one of them sucking on her clit and the other one sucking at her hole. She knew this was going to be it—the orgasm that was so violent she wouldn't be able to stifle her scream.

Oh damn, she thought. She'd managed to make it this far and…

Kieran's mouth unlatched from her clit. His head bobbed up. "Did you hear that?" he whispered.

Alasdair released her pussy. "Kerick's back!"

"Shit! Let's get out of here!"

Tears of mingled fear and frustration welled up in Nellie's eyes. Fear because Kerick was no doubt the name of the man who'd kidnapped her. Frustration because she'd been left on the brink of a violent orgasm and been offered no completion.

She could feel her swollen pussy throbbing, needing release. She felt as though she was being driven mad.

Nellie's eyes flicked open when the boys fled the chamber. She sighed. "What happens now?" she whispered. "What will be done to me?"

Chapter 11

It grew worse instead of better. The tingling between her thighs, the need for satiation—she was going insane, she thought on a low moan.

For the past hour Nellie had laid on the bed of stone and animal hides, her body naked and spread wide, the chill in the air grazing her already erect nipples and swollen clit. Several times she had tried closing her eyes and willing herself to orgasm, but it hadn't been enough. She needed direct stimulation. If only she could free one of her hands...

Footsteps approached, dull thuds on a stone and dirt floor. She swallowed nervously, for she had a fairly good idea who they belonged to. A minute later her suspicion was confirmed when the man she assumed to be named Kerick stormed into the chamber she'd been chained in. And, she thought warily, he looked angry.

"Did they fuck you?" he growled, his nostrils flaring. Three long strides brought him to the slab of stone she'd been stretched out onto. His jaw was tight, his gray eyes murderous. He spread open her cunt lips and checked the size of her hole for recent penetration. *"Did they?"*

Her eyes widened. "N-No," she stuttered.

"Are you lying?" he barked.

Nellie's nostrils did a little flaring of their own. Her gaze flicked down to the hands spreading apart her pussy for inspection, then over the black cloak he wore, then back up to his grim face. "Why would I lie about being raped?" she snapped. Her eyes narrowed at him. "If they'd raped me, I'd want revenge," she spat out meaningfully.

One black eyebrow shot up. He grunted, ignoring the double entendre. "Did they touch you?"

She hesitated. "Yes." She decided he'd know if she was lying.

"Where?" he ground out.

"Everywhere."

His nostrils flared further. "They will be punished," he promised on a low murmur.

As if remembering for the first time that she was lying there naked, stretched out for his use on a slab of stone, his eyelids grew heavy as he stared down at her splayed flesh. His fingers rubbed over her cunt lips, gently massaging them until her breath caught and she felt her nipples stiffen again. When her breasts began to heave up and down in arousal, he placed the pad of his thumb against her clit and applied agonizingly hedonistic pleasure in a circular motion. She gasped.

Sweet Cyrus, Nellie thought on a moan, she didn't want to orgasm for the very man who had kidnapped her. But those boys—they had worked her up into a fit of arousal, and then left her uncompleted. She'd been a step away from climaxing before her abductor had even entered the stone chamber. Now that he was here and stroking her clit...

"Please," she whimpered, her lower back arching.

His eyelids grew impossibly heavier. "Good girl," he said thickly. His intense steel gaze never once left her face as he watched her writhe and moan about on the slab of stone. He increased the pressure, rubbing her clit harder. "Come for me, little one."

She would have given anything to have been able to disobey him, to have been able to deny him the satisfaction of making her orgasm a mere three minutes after he'd entered the chamber, but her body had a mind of its own. And it wanted to come.

"*Oh god.*" Nellie screamed as her nipples stabbed upward, then groaned long and loud as her orgasm jolted though her belly. Her hips instinctively rocked back and forth, giving her as much friction on her clit as was possible.

When the intensity began to wane, when she was once again aware of her surroundings, she warily looked up, her gaze clashing with his.

"They will definitely be punished," he said hoarsely. "No man but me will ever touch you again."

Nellie blinked. She'd forgotten that before her captor had brought her to peak, they had been discussing the fact that the teenage boys had been touching her without permission. She nibbled on her lower lip. They were just boys. In a world where any male higher than she was in the Hierarchy was allowed to play with her body at will, she didn't see the harm in a couple of teenagers wanting to see and feel what a naked woman looked like. "They were just curious," she said quietly. "They didn't hurt me."

A tic began to work in his jaw. "You would defend them?" he growled.

"I wouldn't defend any of you," she hissed. "Least of all you!"

He ignored her not so subtle reprimand. Releasing her labial lips, he stood up, his eyes flicking over her nude body. He studied her broodingly for a long moment, one palm running gently over her belly, then higher to graze over her nipples.

His dark head came up. His eyes found hers. "You can't escape me, Nellie," he softly vowed. "Even if you ran, even if you somehow managed to get away from me for a time, I'd always find you." His gaze flicked down to her breasts, then back up to her face. "But then, you know that already…don't you?"

She looked away, refusing to answer. She knew the truth, of course. He'd proven the validity of his claim when he'd disarmed her sector's security system just to steal her away. But that didn't mean she had to respond to his question.

Silence filled the cold stone chamber. For a long moment Kerick said nothing, though she could feel his eyes boring possessively into her.

"I grant you five hours time to come to terms with your fate, Nellie," he at last murmured, ending the quiet. "There is something I must see to, but I will return for you."

There was a pause and then she asked warily, "What exactly *is* my fate?"

The pad of his thumb lightly grazed the tip of one nipple. She shuddered. "In five hours time I will return for you. You will be waiting for me," he informed her, his voice thick with arousal. "And you will be both welcoming and compliant."

She took a deep breath. Her eyes closed briefly. "You mean to claim me as your sexual chattel then?" she whispered.

His hand stilled on her breast. "I would have thought that much was obvious."

Her head whipped around. She narrowed her eyes at him. "Do not mock me," she gritted out. "I meant that I have a career—I have a life!" she snapped. She looked away, refusing to make eye contact. "And you've taken everything away from me," she whispered. "And for what? To what end? To have a sexual plaything," she said bitterly, answering her own question.

He took her chin in his hand and gently nudged her face to look at him. "You belong to me now, Nellie." His harsh features didn't even waver, didn't show any sign of weakness or a willingness to let her go. "Now *I* am your life."

Her nostrils flared at his arrogance. What made his arrogance that much worse was the fact that she honestly didn't think he was trying to be a jerk—he simply wanted her and to his way of thinking that was just that. "You have no idea what you've just done," she bit out.

"Oh?" One dark eyebrow rose. "Were you the mistress of a leader in the Hierarchy? Do you think he will come here to find you?" His laughter was bitter, angry. She could surmise he didn't much care for any talk of her being intimate with another man, which she found odd. She'd thought all males realized that females rarely to never came to them as virgins. "I promise you, little one, that you will never be found. The weak males of the Hierarchy would never survive outside the protection of a biosphere."

Nellie gasped. Her eyes clashed with Kerick's. "We are…" She wet her lips. "We are on—on the…*Outside*?" Good god, she thought in a panic, any number of horrid things could happen to them outside the protection of the biosphere's perimeter. They could be killed by mutant animals—or worse by sub-humans. "I d-demand that you take me back," she stammered out in a wild voice. "Sweet Cyrus, but why would you sentence the lot of us to death!"

For the first time since she'd known him, she could have sworn his eyes gentled a bit. Just a bit. "I take care of my possessions," he said in low tones. "You have nothing to fear, Nellie."

She snorted at that. "How comforting," she said acidly.

"So as I said," he continued, his eyes narrowed, "your lover will never find you."

Nellie sighed. She shook her head slightly. "I don't have a lover."

Now it was Kerick who did the snorting.

Her jaw clenched. "Don't you think I'd tell you if I did? Holy Cyrus, but I'd love to make you as angry as possible," she gritted out.

Strangely, that appeased him. She could have sworn she'd seen one side of his mouth curl upward in an awkward semi-smile for a threadbare moment before he stifled the reaction and wore his stone façade once again.

Nellie blinked. Had she actually made the grim giant…smile?

She sighed. Why should she give a yen if she had?

"If you have no lover," Kerick rumbled out, his large hands palming her breasts and gently kneading them, "then why did you say I had no idea what I'd just done?"

Stubbornly, she refused to answer him. She harrumphed instead and looked away.

"You will answer me. Now."

She bit down onto her tongue as hard as she could to keep from screaming at his arrogance. Again, she didn't think he was *trying* to be an arrogant jerk because he'd gentled his voice in a way that said her reply mattered to him, but nevertheless the man had the social manners of a hybrid pig let loose at an elegant techno-opera party. She had to keep remembering that he had the upper hand here. For now.

"Nellie…" he warned.

She lay there for a protracted moment feeling petulant, refusing to answer. But she could feel his eyes boring into her as he stood beside her with an inhuman patience waiting for her to answer. She sighed. "I was developing a serum," she quietly admitted. "And I was close to perfecting it."

His large hands stilled on her breasts. "A serum?" He paused. "What kind of a serum?" he murmured.

Nellie's forehead wrinkled at the way he'd asked the question. He actually sounded interested in her answer, which was more than she could say about any other male she'd ever known. Typically the only time a male ever discussed her career with her was to give her his opinion on how selfish she was to keep one. "Sub-humans," she said quietly. She shrugged dismissively, but the gesture was far from casual. "My mother was…infected." She looked away, refusing to say more.

There was a long pause.

"We will discuss this at a later date," Kerick said softly. His palms cupped her breasts and kneaded them. "After you've come to accept your place as my possession."

Nellie's head flew to the side. Her gaze clashed with his. "Why? Why me? Why did you steal me and not another woman?" Her nostrils flared. There had to be more to this than mere sexual longing. "Were you sent by the Hierarchy to murder me?" she gritted out. "Because if you were I'd prefer to get it over with *before* you fuck me."

Another long pause.

"Why would they want you dead?" he asked softly.

It dawned on her what she'd just said to him, what she'd just told him in so many words. Her eyes widened at her own stupidity. How could she have given away so much information? Stupid! Stupid! "I—I..." She glanced away. "I was only jesting," she lied.

Silence filled the cold stone chamber.

"Your skin is chilled," Kerick at last murmured, dismissing her earlier remarks. A single finger traced the outline of an erect nipple.

She blew out a breath. Relief that he hadn't pressed for an explanation? Arousal at being touched so intimately? She no longer knew. "I am," she quietly admitted.

He released her breasts and pulled a small virtual computer device from the pocket of his black cloak. Three button sequences later, the locks on her legs unclicked, freeing them. A second after that she felt the chain that held her arms pinioned above her head give way. She cried out when her arms fell down to her sides, pain jolting through them as they came back to life.

Kerick sat down beside her and began to gently work the knots out of first her arms and then her legs. She averted her gaze the entire time, uncertain what to do or say.

"So long as you are a good girl and do not disobey me, I permit you to wander the length of both this stone chamber as well as the large underground dirt chamber most adjacent to the doors." He waved a hand toward the doors in question. "But you are to go no further. The other five chambers that comprise the catacombs we dwell in are off limits for the time being."

Nellie's eyes flicked around the stone chamber she'd been sequestered in. She sighed. Where was Cabel Modem when a woman in distress needed him? "There's not even a comfortable pillow-bed to sleep on," she grumbled. Given the fact that not having a pillow-bed to sleep on was the least of her problems, she wasn't even sure why she cared, but there it was.

Kerick finished working a large knot out of her arm, then stood up. "I've seen to it that we will have a comfortable pallet for sleeping." Her lips turned down at the word *we*. "But for now I must go. I will return to you in five hours time. Until then, feel free to wander the two chambers." His eyes narrowed. "But do not venture beyond the dirt chamber, Nellie. Be a good girl while I'm gone."

She gritted her teeth at his usage of the word *girl*. That was the second time he'd called her thusly. He truly did have the social manners of a hybrid pig. Had the man been raised in a damn cave? Oh that's right, she thought on a sigh, they were on the Outside. He probably *had* been raised in a cave. Sweet Cyrus.

She turned her head to look at him. His fingers idly sifted through her mane of dark red hair.

"I will not remove the sensory collars," he informed her, dashing her last hope of escape. "You will wear them always that you might remember who it is your body belongs to," he said thickly. His brooding eyes flicked once more over the length of her nude body, his gaze openly hungry.

As then, as if he'd just remembered a prior engagement, he abruptly stood up to take his leave of her. "Five hours," he reminded her, his voice once again steeled and in command. "I grant you but five hours. It's best if you use them wisely."

"Oh? And what do you consider a wise use of my time? Thinking of ways to pleasure you?" she asked bitterly.

He shrugged. "I admit the idea pleases me."

Her jaw dropped open as she watched him walk toward the stone doors. She couldn't believe the man's arrogance. "By what name do I call you?" she ground out. She knew his name, of course, but she wanted to hear him confirm it.

Kerick stopped when he reached the stone doors. He turned his dark head to look at her, his intense gray eyes finding hers. "Master," he murmured. "Your permanent one."

Chapter 12

"Kalast? How in the name of Cyrus did the wench ever make it to Kalast?" Kerick rumbled out the question to Elijah as he helped him transfer the unconscious woman they'd just stolen from the Altun Ha biosphere to the black land conveyance the trio had "borrowed".

Xavier raised an eyebrow. "I must have missed something vital to the conversation, amigos. How could the woman be on Kalast if we're stealing her away for Elijah to master even now?"

Kerick grunted. "Not this woman," he rumbled out. "Elijah was referring to that Karen Williams wench whose name keeps coming up on the virtual memory searches we ran."

Xavier's lips formed an O.

"Don't know how she escaped Earth," Elijah admitted as the trio took their places inside the rough terrain land conveyance. He jumped in behind them from the top of the vehicle before sealing the overhead entrance. "But she obviously had some help from within the Hierarchy, amigo."

Kerick's eyes narrowed in thought as Elijah engaged the land conveyance. The vehicle ignited and took off, hovering a few inches above the ground. "I wonder why she ran," he murmured.

"Dunno." Elijah's mouth, which was typically as glowering as Kerick's, curved upward in a slight smile. "And for tonight at least I don't give a yen."

Xavier snorted at that. "I don't want to hear about it. The two of you already have wenches to master and the best I can do is visit a droid Pussy Parlour," he muttered. "I haven't felt a real pussy in over ten years. Ten years! And when I finally break outta Kong, what do I get? Droid cunt. Very unfair, amigos."

Elijah's deep laughter echoed throughout the conveyance. Kerick's eyes twinkled good-naturedly but he didn't smile. "The Auctioneer will bring in a new crop of wives to bid on in a month's time. You'll have a better selection to choose from then, my friend."

"Shit, Riley," Xavier mumbled, "my cock will have fallen off by then." His head came up as he glanced at Kerick. "You sure you won't share? It's done all the time in poor households amongst brothers." He shrugged his shoulders. "Growing up, my own mother called five men master. My father and all four of my uncles."

Kerick's jaw tensed. He didn't like the idea of other males looking at Nellie, let alone sharing her body with them. Not even a friend who was practically a brother. "I don't share."

Xavier heard the subtle warning in his tone. He nodded once, dismissing the subject. "In a month then."

The males were silent for the next twenty minutes while the conveyance ventured toward the biosphere's perimeter. This was the tricky part, steering out of it without setting off any security devices within Altun Ha. Tricky, but not impossible. Indeed, they had already made this trip from the biosphere to the catacombs seven times since they'd escaped. This was the eighth time.

The seventh trip to the biosphere was, in Kerick's estimation, the best yielding one for it had been the same occasion that he'd unmanned the security system to reach Nellie — Nellie Kan.

And, as it turned out, *Doctor* Nellie Kan.

He had wanted her from the moment he'd broken into Vorice Henders' office chamber looking for information, but had ended up viewing Nellie through the sensory cameras instead. He had thought her a lab technician or perhaps a protégée for she had looked young to him. But no — as it turned out she was a full-fledged scientist within the Hierarchy who had seen thirty-two years.

Kerick had watched through the sensory cameras that night as Nellie had stripped off her clothing. He had lusted for her as he'd never lusted a woman in his life when she'd bent over into the laboratory closet, searching for—whatever it was she had been searching for. And when she had turned around and started playing with her tits and pussy...

He had known then and there that he would steal her away. Those large, heavy breasts, her ruby red nipples, and that rare breed of dark red hair—the sort of female he'd spent fifteen years in Kong fantasizing about owning.

Now he owned her, he thought possessively.

Kerick had decided upon stealing Nellie away that same night he'd viewed her through the sensory cameras, but she had thwarted him. Unknowingly on her part, most likely.

It had been fifteen plus years since he'd been within touching distance of a human woman, so seeing Nellie, smelling her scent, hearing her voice—it had shaken him enough to make him momentarily forget what he'd set out to do. By the time he'd mastered his wits, she'd been halfway to the atrium.

That evening he had cursed himself an idiot for allowing her to escape him so easily. It was a fact that would eventually inflame him, for getting to her after that had been no small feat. That night in the lab she had been easy pickings. But from that evening onward, she had been careful, very aware of her surroundings while coming and going, often having an armed guard escort her to and from the atrium.

Finally, not knowing what else to do, and desperate to keep her away from other males after having watched those Hierarchical scientists touch all over her body at the Fathom Systems party, Kerick had decided on taking her by force—at home. Elijah and Xavier had called him mad, but he'd ignored them and carried through with the course he'd set for himself just as he always did.

It had paid off. Nellie was in the catacombs even now. And she was all his.

"There's something I forgot to mention to you," Xavier said, ending the silence.

Kerick arched an eyebrow but said nothing.

"About that female named Karen who escaped to Kalast..."

"Yes?"

"She was a scientist within the Hierarchy when she fled."

Kerick's body stilled. "You are certain?"

"Very." Xavier frowned. "The virtual memory searches I ran were conclusive. I don't know what that means, if it means anything at all, but for some reason the correlation doesn't sit well with me."

"Nor with me," Kerick murmured. He thought back on Nellie, and how in a moment of fright and anger she had accused him of being an assassin for the Hierarchy. She had believed her own words without a doubt. Which meant that she had been expecting to die. Just like his mother had been expecting to die back when he'd been a small boy.

The question, of course, was why? What did she know?

"You better get your female to talk," Elijah warned. "She might know something without even realizing it."

Kerick inclined his head. Half of what Elijah had said was correct — Nellie probably did know something. But the other half of Elijah's sentence was most likely false — Nellie not only knew something, but she was aware of what that something was. "She'll talk," he rumbled out.

Xavier grinned. "Awfully sure of yourself, amigo."

"I am." Kerick stared straight ahead, his grim features concealed in the shadows. "It just means I shall have to master her sooner than I expected to is all."

Elijah looked doubtful. "Not sure that's possible, old friend, or even recommendable. Females are like pets — takes time and a lot of patience on your part for them to trust you enough to allow themselves to grow dependent on you."

"Under normal circumstances, perhaps." Kerick hated the harsh tactics he knew he'd have to use to bring Nellie to heel, but it was necessary. Her life might depend upon it. All of their lives might depend upon it.

Tonight he would greedily fuck her as many times as her body could handle, but tomorrow, in the morning, her mastering would begin. "But then these circumstances are not precisely normal," he murmured.

Chapter 13

AND ALWAYS, NIGHT AND DAY, HE WAS IN
THE MOUNTAINS AND IN THE TOMBS, CRYING, AND
CUTTING HIMSELF WITH STONES...

Stones.

Of course.

Nellie's teeth sank down into her lower lip. Her eyes widened as comprehension slowly dawned. Margaret Riley was, if nothing else, too clever for her own good. She'd hidden her analogies well, had used ancient religious text to throw any potential and unwelcomed journal thieves off the scent, but they were there as plain as a summer day in the Scandinavian biospheres are long if you knew what it was you were looking for.

Problem was, Nellie thought on a sigh, for the most part she still didn't know what she was looking for. Clues, yes, but clues to what?

For years she had believed that the worn diary would help her unravel how the sub-human had come into existence, which would help her create an effective serum. And although she still believed the journal held the key to the answers she sought, she now understood that Dr. Riley had been trying to tell her more. But what more?

She closed her eyes briefly, not wanting to deal with the implications of her suspicions. If what she was beginning to suspect was accurate, then it was very possible, in fact probable, that the journal not only answered the question of how sub-humans had been infected, but why…and worse yet, by whom.

And Jesus said unto him, Come out of the man, thou unclean spirit.

And he asked him, What is thy name? And the demon answered, saying, My name is Legion, for we are many.

"Do you really want to know the answer, Nellie?" she whispered to herself. She brought her knees up and wrapped her arms around them, the stone pallet underneath her feeling cold against her naked buttocks.

She might be a captive today, she thought, but there was always tomorrow and with it a new chance to flee. By continuing her study of Dr. Riley's journal when she did escape, by purposely seeking out the answers she knew the diary held, she would, in effect, be changing the course of her existence forever. She would always be on the run, just as

Margaret Riley had been. She would be forced to remain in the frightening Outside world, a place where the only laws were the ones violent outlaws and equally dangerous sub-humans had created for themselves. She would —

Sweet Cyrus, nothing would ever be the same again. The chip, the sub-humans, the Hierarchy — somehow all connected.

Nellie took a deep breath and expelled it, her hand idly sifting through her mane of dark red hair. If she didn't do the right thing, she'd never be able to look at herself in the image map again. But if she did...well, she might not be alive long enough to do anything about the answers she dug up.

One thing was for certain, she thought as she glanced around the stone chamber she'd been thrown into: she had to get out of here. Now.

AND ALWAYS, NIGHT AND DAY, HE WAS IN THE MOUNTAINS AND IN THE TOMBS, CRYING, AND CUTTING HIMSELF WITH STONES...

"The zida stone," she whispered, her eyes round.

Nellie's heartbeat picked up rapidly and went into overdrive. A small smile tugged at the corners of her lips when the first piece of the puzzle clicked definitively into place.

The zida stone was a rare and costly gem strewn throughout the catacombs and mines of a few South American biospheres. The rock was not indigenous to Earth, for in reality it wasn't actually a gem but the scattered remains of a felled meteorite that had been blown to bits by the Hierarchy about forty years past.

Not much was known about the zida stone by the average scientist, for none would be so bold as to venture out of the perimeter of a biosphere to obtain and study one, but a few facts were known about it amongst Nellie's peers. Only a few, she realized, but they were important.

She stood up, hands on her hips while she paced, trying to remember the exact wording of the lecture Treymor Lorin had given her concerning the zida stone.

She sat on his lap naked, her back to his chest, her legs spread open, the fingertips of his right hand sifting through the triangle of dark red curls covering her mons. His fingers went lower, pressing against her clit, making her gasp. The two scientists who sat opposite Dr. Lorin chuckled, grateful to him for providing a show with a rare human female for their viewing pleasure.

"Ride me," he whispered in her ear before licking it. "My friends have traveled all the way

from Biosphere 5 just to watch me fuck a real female." His free hand moved aside the silken white robe he wore, exposing his penis. He nudged Nellie's buttocks with the tip, telling her without words to impale herself on him.

Eighteen-years-old, and naively trusting of her mentor, she'd unquestioningly done what he'd wanted her to do. Raising her hips, she sank down onto his cock with a groan, impaling herself to the hilt.

She tried not to blush when, in a moment of lust, a seventy-year-old scientist began pulling at her young nipples and laughing while he told her to ride Dr. Lorin harder so her breasts would jiggle for him. She tried to feel no embarrassment when his colleague, a scientist of approximately fifty, stood up and stuffed his cock into her mouth.

"Suck on me," the fifty-year-old scientist groaned in a thick Irish lilt. He was dangerously close to coming already, his fingers threading through the hair on her head. "Oh yes, Nellie, what a good girl you are…"

Dr. Lorin's fingers painfully dug into the flesh of her hips, a reminder that she had better not forget to pleasure him as well. Still sucking on the scientist's cock while feeling her nipples get tugged on by the other one, she slammed her hips down hard and rode Dr. Lorin as fast as she could.

Her breasts jiggled up and down as she rode him, making the seventy-year-old hiss with pleasure as he watched the soft globes bounce up and down. He tweaked at her nipples harder.

Dr. Lorin made a soft purring sound, then continued his lecture while she fucked him. "The properties of a zida stone…

1. *The inside of the charcoal gray zida stone is said to contain a milky gray substance with a highly hallucinogenic solution.*
2. *The hallucinogenic solution is believed to be indigenous to the planet Xiom, a trader world on the eastern cusp of the Vega Star System, where the wilds of the mountains are so dangerous that not even native lifeforms will explore it.*
3. *The density of the zida stone is quite heavy, for when the rocks first hit the Earth's surface, they sunk below ground and ended up in catacombs and mines…"*

And that, Nellie thought, her breath catching in the back of her throat as she continued to pace the chamber, brought her to point number 4:

Nellie drained the fifty-year-old scientist's cock of sperm with her mouth, the sound of his gasps echoing throughout the terrace as she drank him dry. Dr. Lorin clutched her hips, his fingers imprinting the flesh there as he came on a loud groan, emptying himself of seed inside of her pussy.

"And," he panted, taking a kerchief from his robe and mopping his brow with it, that brings me to the final property of a zida stone…

4. *A strong magnetic force surrounds the outside of a zida stone, one so powerful that*

any electrically charged and/or radio-wave induced communications device within twenty feet of its position becomes shifty at best and non-effective at worst..."

Her eyes flicked down to the sensory chains she wore, sensory chains that had been programmed using the most advanced electrical and radio-wave technology.

Advanced or not, she thought, her heartbeat thumping madly, a zida stone could polarize it.

Her eyes flicked toward the doors. She nibbled on her lower lip.

It was her only shot. She needed to escape. And, she thought as she slowly made her way across the stone chamber, she needed Margaret Riley's journal back in her hands.

Nellie opened the doors quietly, her head poking out to ascertain if she was being watched. Sensing that the coast was clear, she was careful to make as little sound as possible as she inched her way out into the corridor.

Grabbing a lit torch from off of a nearby wall sconce, she kept her eyes alert for hybrid animal activity as she made her way deeper into the bowels of the Earth.

It was time to explore the adjacent dirt chamber.

* * * * *

"Steady," Kerick murmured, his eyes never straying from the pack of sub-humans surrounding them. "Keep it nice and steady, amigos."

Xavier swallowed a bit roughly. "I think I just shit myself," he muttered.

Elijah softly snorted at that as his grip tightened around the flash-stick he'd palmed when they'd first been ambushed. The land conveyance had short-circuited, leaving the group no choice but to trek through the jungle by foot. The woman he'd stolen began to quietly cry, so he drew her closer against his side with his free arm. "Give the word when you're ready, Riley," he said under his breath.

Kerick's gaze remained fixed on the largest of the creatures, the female he assumed to be the pack's leader. Her deadly black claws were fully visible, one spiking up from the tip of each finger. Her fangs were bared, indicating her hunger. A thick, viscous saliva frothed from the naked female's mouth, dripping down her chin and between her breasts. The crimson pupils in her slate black eyes held no warmth, no compassion or pity, no guilt.

But the rest of her looked as human as she'd once been. And that, Kerick admitted to himself, was what made killing a sub-human so difficult. This female had been infected by no fault of her own; indeed some human somewhere was probably mourning the loss of her still to this day, so much wanting their mother — or sister — or daughter — back, yet knowing in their heart that eventually she would die. Like this.

Did my mother die like this?

Kerick's eyes gentled with pity, even as he took a deep breath and opened his mouth to give the command that would sentence these creatures to death. His gaze flicked from the large female toward a smaller female child who looked to be no more than ten. Either the Hierarchy had purposely infected her or she'd wandered off from her family's domicile and gotten bitten by a sub-human, but either way the pathetic creature would never live to see another tomorrow. His nostrils flared at the injustice of it all.

Steeling himself against his emotions, and mollifying himself with the promise of retribution on behalf of those that would die today, Kerick aimed one brief nod in Elijah and Xavier's direction. "Let's do it, amigos," he murmured.

Xavier closed his eyes briefly, expelled a deep breath, then nodded back. "I got your back, old friend."

Three feet away, a low growling sound emitted from the little girl's throat as fangs exploded through her gums. Screaming the most horrific, blood-curdling sound imaginable, she squatted down upon her thighs and lunged long and high through the air, her claws spiking out as she aimed herself bodily towards Kerick.

Kerick sighed as he raised the muscled arm holding a flash-stick high into the air. He'd chosen this weapon as opposed to the others he carried to make certain that the kill was done as quickly and cleanly as possible.

He aimed the flash-stick's sites directly between the little girl's eyes as her body hovered over his head. She whimpered in mid-air, the sight of the weapon triggering a memory of a former life, and a former self.

Their eyes clashed.

Comprehension dawned in the child's gaze.

Kerick's heart constricted.

"Sleep with the angels, querida," he whispered.

* * * * *

Nellie closed her eyes and willed herself to calm down, commanded her breathing to return to normal.

This is no time to lose it, Nellie, she chastised herself. *Calm down. Start over. You can do this. You* have *to do this. The serum has to be finished. You must get out of here and get that journal back.*

She opened her eyes and took a deep breath. Her gaze flicked around the underground dirt chamber. It was a large hollow within the earth, approximately twenty feet high and forty feet across. Three pools bubbled up from pits in the ground, two of them filled with precious mineral water and one with what she assumed to be boiling tar.

She held the torch up as her gaze narrowed at the pit of bubbling black sludge. Her eyes widened in comprehension. "That's not tar," she murmured. She stood up, then walked slowly across the chamber. When she'd reached the bubbling pit, she leaned over, crouching down upon her knees. "Definitely not tar."

The pit, she could surmise, had once been filled with virgin mineral water, just as the other two pits were. But something had caused it to change, to become blackened. Perhaps, she thought as she leaned in closer to the dark pool, perhaps something from the heavens had landed in it, forcing the mineral pool to change. "A meteorite," she whispered.

Nellie took a hard look at the underground chamber surrounding her, asking herself while she did if it was possible this underground hollow she was in had been carved out within the belly of the earth when a chunk of alien meteorite had struck it. "Very possible," she muttered to herself. "In fact, probable."

Her gaze flew wildly about the chamber. There had to be some sort of stick laying around. Or something—anything—she could use to dig into the black sludge with.

Nothing.

Taking a deep breath, she closed her eyes and ordered herself to find the courage to do what needed to be done. She had no idea what the chemical breakdown of the bubbling black pool was, or even the temperature of it, but she knew she had to stick a finger in it regardless, to see if it was temperate enough to place her entire arm in.

A zida stone, or perhaps many zida stones, could be wedged down inside the frothing pit. All it would take was one rock—just one—and her chances at escape would increase a thousandfold.

Her eyes flicked open. She took one more calming breath. "It's now or never, Nellie," she whispered.

Slowly, she lowered her hand toward the bubbling pool. Her heartbeat accelerated and perspiration broke out onto her brow and between her cleavage. She took a deep breath and expelled it, air coming out in a rush, as she quickly dipped her index finger into the bubbling ooze.

Her eyes widened. "It's temperate," she murmured.

Chapter 14

December 23, 2249 A.D.

Kerick couldn't remember ever being more tired. The walk through the jungle had taken hours—hours he could have spent with Nellie. It had been his intention to spend last night giving her endless pleasure and seeking his own in return, but now there was no time left for generosity. He had to get down to the business of mastering her. He had to break her to his will. His encounter with the sub-humans had only further solidified that fact in his mind, for he needed Nellie to talk.

Pulling himself out of the stream he'd been bathing in, he walked toward a hidden break in a nearby boulder that led to the catacombs below. Naked, he crept quietly into the break, stopped long enough to light a torch, then made his way down the rocky dirt path that led into the belly of the Earth.

The sound of a woman moaning made his heart stop. He came to a halt, his eyes narrowed.

It couldn't be Elijah and his newly acquired female making all that noise, for

Elijah had taken his wench down into a deeper chamber, the same one he'd lived in for years whenever they'd had "business" to see to near the Altun Ha biosphere.

The moaning grew louder, causing Kerick's nostrils to flare. The voices, he surmised, were coming from the chamber he'd placed Nellie in. Enraged, he walked quickly toward where the sound was coming from, his muscles cording in preparation of a fight.

He would kill Xavier with his own two hands if he was fucking Nellie, he silently vowed. He'd gut him. Flay him. Strangle—

He stopped abruptly when he reached the stone chamber. His gray eyes widened fractionally. Where in the name of Cyrus was Nellie?

There were but two occupants within the stone chamber and neither of them was the woman Kerick had stolen for himself. His eighteen-year-old brother Kieran was one of the people in the chamber, and the young boy was greedily sucking the cunt of a gorgeous tied up blonde female who looked to be in her late thirties.

One corner of his mouth lifted in a small smile. He could gather from the fact that the wench wore no nipple chains—yet—that she was unmarried. Which meant the female had managed to make it for close to forty years before getting hunted down and claimed as a male's possession.

Now she was a possession. His brother's property.

Kerick shook his head and walked away, a grin tugging at his lips. Apparently after young Kieran has tasted Nellie—an occurrence he still got angry about when he thought on it—the boy had decided to go out and find a pussy of his own to lick and fuck. Kerick could well imagine what Xavier's reaction would be when he found out, which was why the grin. The thirty-six-year-old Xavier had made a direct path for the first droid Pussy Parlour available when they'd come out of the jungle, while eighteen-year-old Kieran was about to get the real thing.

Kerick made his way toward the dirt chamber, assuming it to be where he'd find Nellie. His cock stiffened at the thought of being inside of her, at the knowledge that after fifteen years of sexual deprivation he would finally be able to sink his manhood into a warm, welcoming cunt.

He hoped the beautiful scientist had spent the hours-long reprieve she'd been given to come to terms with her fate. She belonged to him now, she would always belong to him, and Kerick would never give her up.

After he buried himself balls-deep inside of her, he'd get her pregnant. And then, he thought, his cock stiffening all the more, he'd be permitted by the laws of the Underground to chain her nipples.

Then they would be official. And everyone would know she irrevocably belonged to him.

* * * * *

She prided herself on her cunning, on her ability to slip in and out of potentially threatening situations. When she had left the Underground safe haven of Xibalba, which was a network of ancient catacombs within the bowels of the Earth that learned females used to go into hiding within, she had done so with the intent of quickly slipping in to help Dr. Kan escape, then to quickly slip back out with none the wiser.

But Dr. Kan had apparently escaped before she'd even shown up. Either that or the scientist was being hidden away in a chamber she hadn't yet located.

And then the unthinkable had happened. She, a ten-year veteran of *locate-and-rescue* operations—and a lifelong veteran of throwing males of the species off her trail—had been captured.

She couldn't believe it. After thirty-seven years of managing to thwart the efforts of every male who had ever sought to claim her, she had finally been caught. And worse, she had been captured and claimed by a teenage boy who'd tracked her down with a cunning she hadn't thought males possible of.

Sweet Cyrus.

She groaned when yet another orgasm tore through her belly. Gasping for air, her eyes flew open and her gaze trailed down to where the boy—Kieran—was sucking on her pussy. Her clit was so sensitive she felt like it would explode if her captor didn't stop toying with it. Her nipples were so stiff that she feared even the softest of touches would be painful.

But he didn't stop—he never stopped. He sucked on her pussy again and again, wringing orgasms out of her that were so intense as to be painful. She could tell he was a virgin, knew that he'd never fucked a female before. His eyes were closed in bliss as he lapped at her, growls of pleasure erupting from his drenched mouth as he kept his face buried between her thighs for the better part of an hour.

By the time he was finished, by the time Kieran had sucked her pussy to his heart's content, she was a writhing, moaning, gasping, convulsing, half-hysterical female in dire need of being fucked. Whomever it was that had lectured to this boy on the ways of mastering had known what he was about.

He raised his dark head from between her legs. Panting, she watched as his handsome face bobbed into her line of vision. Their gazes clashed.

She watched in helplessness, in lust, as Kieran grabbed his swollen cock by the base and guided the tip toward her opening. Her nipples stiffened even more just from seeing the look of awe on his face, hearing the way he gasped when he slid the head inside of her wet cunt.

"Sweet Cyrus," he moaned.

"Go deeper," she heard herself whisper. "Slide all the way inside of me."

On a groan he complied, his heavy-lidded eyes squeezing all the way shut as he sank his young swollen cock into her pussy all the way to the hilt. His breath came out in a hiss as he began to move, his teeth gritting as he slowly stroked all the way in and all the way out of her flesh.

Her eyelids grew heavy. She shuddered when he lowered his face to her breasts and began licking her nipples as he continued to slowly thrust in and out of her body. "Faster," she gasped. She put her needs into terms she was certain even a naïve boy could understand. "If you want my pussy to make more juice for you, you have to fuck me faster."

He moaned from in between her cleavage, his heavy head coming to rest on her large breasts as his fingers played with her nipples. He continued to thrust slowly in and out of her, his eyes closed tightly. "I don't want to," he said shakily. "If I go faster my cock will spurt. I want it to last."

Sweet Cyrus, she thought, she'd never before considered how lust-provoking a virgin male could be. His face was pillowed on her breasts, so she could only see one side of it, but the view was enough to allow her to glimpse the dreamy expression on her captor's face. He looked as though he'd died and gone to the heavens.

Even the way his innocent fingers plucked at her nipples was a turn-on. He played with them intently, as if they were two new toys he'd just acquired and would never let go of. And then there was the slow, heady, mind-numbing sex he was giving to her...the expression writ across his face said it all: he wanted to savor every stroke.

She, on the other hand, was being driven insane.

"It's okay if you spurt," she whispered. She wished she wasn't tied up. Not only because it would make escaping easier, but perversely, because she also had a mad urge to run her fingers through his dark hair. "Your cock will stiffen up again and make more juice to shoot inside of me."

He raised his head from her chest and trustingly met her gaze. "Are you certain?"

Holy Kalast but she was certain. "Yes," she said thickly. She wet her lips. "I'm certain."

Kieran cupped her breasts as best he could, and then settled his large body atop hers. "I love you," he said with heart-wrenching innocence, almost making her feel guilty for planning to run from him. "I'm so glad I captured you."

She took a deep breath and expelled it. He was too young to separate affairs of the heart from affairs of the flesh, so would it kill her to give him back the words his expression said he was desperate to hear?

"I love you too," she murmured, her heart squeezing at the look of joy on his face. "And I'm glad that if I had to be claimed, it was by you." That, at least, was the truth.

Kieran grinned down at her as he rotated his hips and slid the head of his eager penis inside of her flesh. A moment later his expression turned serious when he sank into her pussy balls-deep on a groan.

He fucked her long and hard, moaning and groaning while he pounded in and out of her cunt, greedily filling her up with his swollen cock. He came quickly the first time, and again the second time, but he never stopped his fast, hard thrusting.

When she finally came for him, when her flesh began to contract around him and milk him of more seed, he somehow knew this was the last time he'd be able to come—for now. Squeezing his eyes tightly shut, he picked up the pace of his thrusting and crammed his cock harder and deeper and faster into her flesh.

He growled as he burst, frenziedly fucking her while his balls drained of cum.

A few minutes later, when they'd both come down from their mutual high and after he had removed the ropes that had bound her hands over her head, Kieran was too exhausted to do anything but sleep. Drowsy, he snuggled his face into her cleavage and popped a nipple into his mouth. He sighed contentedly, his large body pinning her smaller one to the animal hide bed.

She took a deep breath and blew it out, one hand leisurely stroking his mane of midnight-black hair while he slept.

Kieran and Karen. Karen and Kieran.

Holy Cyrus, she thought. They sounded like a singing droid duo.

Chapter 15

The sound of bellowing, of an enraged male losing control, echoed throughout the catacombs.

"What the hell?" Elijah muttered. He sat up, groggily looking around. His female, the imported English wench he'd stolen, slept quietly beside him. He sighed, then stood up and padded out of the chamber.

* * * * *

A popping sound echoed in the stone chamber as Kieran's mouth unlatched from around her nipple. His head shot up from her breasts.

"What's wrong?" Karen asked throatily, her voice thick with arousal.

"Dunno," Kieran admitted as he slid his cock out of her pussy. "But I'll be right back, querida." He grinned down at her before moving off her body.

She bit her lip. "Are you going to tie me up again?"

His eyes gentled, but he was nobody's fool. "Of course," he murmured.

Karen sighed as he went through the motions of securing her to the stone wall—sighing because her escape efforts had been thwarted or because she'd miss the feel of him stuffing his big penis into her while he was gone she was no longer certain.

He ran a large hand over her belly, then over the swell of her breasts. He plucked at a nipple before strolling from the chamber.

Her eyes flicked toward him, studying him as she watched him walk away.

He wouldn't be easy to escape from, she knew. He was young, he was in love, and he'd just claimed a pussy for his own private use.

Sweet Cyrus.

* * * * *

"This had better be good, amigo." Xavier, the first to arrive in the underground dirt chamber, swiped a hand over his stubbled jaw. "I just got back from the Pussy Parlour," he muttered. "Shit I'm tired." When Kerick said nothing, when he simply stood there staring into space, Xavier cocked his head to study him.

Kerick's jaw was tensed, his muscles corded, his nostrils flaring. He looked like he was ready to kill someone. Xavier had never seen him this angry. "Amigo?" he murmured. "What in the name of Cyrus is wrong?"

"She's gone," he gritted out. Kerick's eyes narrowed as he slowly turned his dark head to look at Xavier. "Nellie escaped."

Chapter 16

December 26, 2249 A.D.

Slipping through the hidden console within the image map of her domicile, Nellie dragged herself into the bathing chamber as she tried to catch her breath. Sleeping by day and making her way through the rough terrain of the jungle by night had taken its toll on her both physically and mentally.

She had been on the run for the better part of four consecutive days, missing out on the festive holiday celebration within the biosphere while running for her life on the Outside. Christmas had always been her favorite holiday, so she was feeling melancholy that she'd missed it. Given everything she'd just gone through she wasn't certain why she even cared, but there it was.

She was tired, she thought weakly. She was hungry. She was dirtier than she'd ever before been in her life. And, she thought with a frown, she was also sick to death of being naked. But first things first…

Stepping under the sanitized shower, she instructed the machine to wash her hair, then called for her droid to wash her body. She closed her eyes as Cyrus 12 lathered her all up, running her silver hands up and down her body. Over her breasts, over her belly, then down lower to her mons.

Mmmm, she thought, her eyes closing, *this feels so good.*

She hurt everywhere. She ached everywhere. She'd been scratched up by branches, she'd skinned up her knees on jagged rocks, and she'd been chased down by hybrid animals. The only thing she could be thankful for was the fact that she hadn't run into even a single sub-human throughout the entire four-day trek back to the biosphere. The possibility had terrified her while on the Outside for she had been weaponless, but somehow, through the grace of Cyrus perhaps, she had escaped unscathed.

When the sanitized shower was finished washing her hair, she retired into her large bathing pool and instructed Cyrus 12 to wash it again. It felt incredible to have her hair shampooed—glorious even after having been so dirty for so long. The feel of the droid's fingers expertly massaging her scalp was almost enough to lull her to sleep.

She closed her eyes and smiled as she sank down lower into the heated, bubbling water. "I'm certain you made my excuses to Fathom

Systems rather than telling my employer the truth?" she ventured.

"Affirmative, Dr. Kan. I told them you were feeling unwell."

Nellie nodded. She had expected Cyrus 12 would have the smarts to do so. Suddenly she was thankful she'd spent the extra yen on an advanced model like her droid rather than on one of the cheaper, less intelligent models. "Did anything happen in my absence I should be informed of, Cyrus 12?"

"Affirmative. On the night of your departure, the slave went back online at 2300 hours, approximately twenty hours after the estimated time..."

The droid went on to list every inconsequential detail that had transpired since Nellie had been kidnapped. She sighed, wondering if robotics engineers would ever learn how to make a droid understand the difference between crucial and trivial information. She listened with half an ear while she soaked, her muscles feeling infinitely better thanks to the bubbling mineral water of the pool.

"...and then this morning, at 0813 Zulu time, Vorice Henders and two unidentified males searched your domicile..."

Nellie's eyes flew open. Her heart rate soared.

"...they left at approximately —"

"Halt!" She wiggled out from beneath the droid's shampooing hands and turned to question her. "What are you saying?" she breathed out. She began to tremble. "They searched my domicile?"

"Affirmative."

Sweet Cyrus.

She closed her eyes and took a deep breath. Her eyes flew open and clashed with the droid's. "We have to get out of here," she said shakily. She willed herself to calm down and think rationally, but her gaze rounded as a thought struck her. "Did they find the book?" she whispered.

"To which book are you—"

"The journal," she said firmly. "Dr. Riley's diary."

The droid searched her memory cells. "Negative."

Nellie chewed on her bottom lip as she stood up. "Did they realize you were observing them, Cyrus 12?" It seemed a bit odd that Henders and his men would carry on with their illegal activities right in front of the droid, realizing as they must have that Cyrus 12 would report everything she witnessed back to her mistress. Her programming would allow for nothing less.

"Negative, Dr. Kan," the droid replied in a monotone as she attempted to help Nellie step into a full-length gold silk robe that was in the height of fashion. But Nellie was too busy running into her sleeping chamber to cooperate. The droid followed on her heels. "I was deactivated. The humans believed me to be unaware of their movement."

Well that explained Henders' laissez-faire attitude, she thought as she frantically opened up the secret panel within her pillow-bed. Her sleazy employer must have believed Cyrus 12 to be a cheap model. Less expensive droids didn't host the ability to assimilate information while deactivated, but the more expensive models did. Thank the heavens.

She keyed in her code, then expelled a breath of relief when the mechanism popped open, revealing the diary of Margaret Riley within it. "Thank Cyrus," she muttered as she snatched up the worn book.

She whirled around to face her droid. She felt ready to lose it, ready to collapse from fear and exhaustion, but she knew that she couldn't. If she gave in now, if she even slowed down, the Hierarchy would find her. She couldn't allow for that—not when so much depended upon her survival.

"Listen to me, old friend," Nellie said quietly. She took the droid's hands in her own. "We have to leave and we have to leave now. If we don't, those men will come back and they'll kill us both." She knew it was the truth. They'd short-circuit Cyrus 12 to keep her from telling others what they'd done to Nellie. And Nellie, well, she knew she'd be the first one expunged from existence. "I need you to go dress yourself in a nondescript robe with a hood." She didn't want others to see the droid's face — nothing that could give away who they were. "I'm going to do the same. While I'm gathering supplies I want you to find us some manner of weaponry."

The droid nodded with a perfect human affectation. "As you command, Dr. Kan." She searched her memory cells. "But statistically you have a better chance of survival if you leave without me."

Nellie's heart wrenched. If she left Cyrus 12 behind, she would no doubt be raped and short-circuited beyond repair. She hadn't realized until that moment how much the droid had come to mean to her. "No. I'll take the chance." When Cyrus 12 opened up her mouth to cite more statistics, Nellie held up a palm. "Besides, your memory cells are citing probables that would be true if we were remaining in the biosphere." Her heartbeat picked up dramatically. "But we're going into the jungle," she whispered.

The droid hosted no pre-programmed knowledge of a jungle. "I do not understand this word…"

"The Outside," she said firmly. "Now let's go."

The droid's eyes widened as a human's would. "Statistically, the chances of survival are—"

"Please don't tell me." She turned on her heel and walked quickly to the other side of the sleeping chamber where her body décor had been draped. "I don't want to know as I've already beaten the odds once. Hurry up, Cyrus 12!" she said urgently. "We've got to get out of here. *Now*."

The droid obeyed without further argument, spinning around and making her way to the auto-kitchen to search for make-shift weaponry.

Nellie blew out a breath as she quickly donned a nondescript gray robe, then frantically threw together some supplies. Regardless to whatever statistics her droid might have spewed out, Nellie realized they only had one real shot at surviving. And that shot, she conceded, wasn't even a very good one. It was based upon the words of an infected woman—a female who might have been half delirious when she'd handed Dr. Riley's journal over to Nellie along with her small bit of esoteric advice.

"If ever you find yourself in trouble," the *woman had warned, "look to the Outside and find the Xibalba."*

Nellie blinked. Her brow wrinkled. "The Xibalba? What is—"

The woman's entire body began to tremble. Nellie backed up quickly, fearing a transformation would come upon the informant.

The woman bared her fangs, her body violently shaking. Nellie's hand flew up to her mouth to cover it, for she could tell the older woman was trying her damnedest to fight the insanity off and was losing. Mingled pity and fear welled in her eyes.

"Go to the Outside," the woman rasped as ten black claws jutted up from the tips of her fingers. She cried out as she gazed down at her trembling hands surrealistically, her expression horrified as blood dripped from the puncture wounds the claws had made when stabbing up from below the skin. She slowly backed away, preparing to flee before she did Nellie harm. "Look to the jungle and you will find the Xibalba."

Nellie watched as the older woman launched herself into the air and fled away into the night. She clutched the journal against her chest and took a deep breath, steadying herself.

Xibalba — the ancient Mayan word for Underworld...

The Xibalba was not real, she thought. Its existence was but a rumor, no doubt concocted by disgruntled females wishing to escape the horror of their everyday existence. An underground network run by learned women? No, it couldn't be real.

Could it?

Running back toward the bathing chamber to disappear through the image map, she stopped for a moment to take a long hard look at her sleeping chamber. Cyrus 12 said nothing, just watched Nellie mourn the loss of the life she had worked so hard to attain.

Years of hard work, years of diligent study and sacrifice...

It had taken all Nellie had to give and more to buy the domicile, the one place on Earth that had been all her own. Her eyes stung with tears that she refused to let fall.

She knew in her heart that she would never lay eyes on her home again.

* * * * *

"Well?" Kerick barked. "Did you discover any useful information?" His steel gray eyes tracked Xavier's movements as his friend alighted inside of the stolen land conveyance and sealed the overhead entrance.

"She definitely hasn't been back to Fathom Systems," Xavier said on a sigh. His features were grim. "Amigo, I think you better accept the possibility that—"

"They have not killed her," Kerick ground out. His jaw tightened. He *hoped* they had not killed her was more to the point, but he refused to allow himself to consider the possibility. If she was dead, he would never forgive himself.

Kerick had realized that Nellie was in danger from the moment she'd admitted to being a scientist within the Hierarchy. He should never have left her alone.

At the time he had thought it was the honorable thing to do—Elijah had aided him in deactivating the sector's security so he could steal away Nellie for his own, and so he had returned the favor for his old friend that Elijah might have the woman he coveted as well. He had even done as much before he'd had the opportunity to claim Nellie sexually, which was an activity his body raged from the need of. Aiding Elijah had seemed honorable at the time. Now it just seemed stupid.

"What do you want to do now?" Xavier asked as he steered the hovering land conveyance over the harsh jungle terrain.

Kerick pondered that question for a long moment. His eyes narrowed determinedly. "Return to the catacombs," he answered. It was the logical place to start. "I want to see if there has been any Underground whispers about a red-headed female scientist on the run."

The familiar mix of anger at Nellie for disobeying him mingled with worry for her safety knotted in his gut. He needed to hunt her, needed to get her back. When he claimed her this time, he'd see to it that the deed was done properly. He'd master her quickly, gain her trust and dependency, and from there he would be able to help her. He'd be able to help them all.

Kerick sighed heavily as his gaze flicked toward the wild jungle terrain outside of the conveyance.

If Nellie was out there he would find her.

He only prayed that he found her before the Hierarchy did.

* * * * *

Next in the serial:

DEATH ROW:
THE HUNTER

ISBN # 1-84360-368-3

In this installment: Kerick recaptures Nellie in a reunion you won't soon forget; Elijah, Xavier, and Kerick plot the demise of the Hierarchy; Kieran begins to suspect there is more to the woman he claimed than meets the eye.

Ellora's Cave Publishing
www.ellorascave.com

About the author:

Critically acclaimed Jaid Black is the best-selling author of numerous erotic romance tales. Her first title, *The Empress' New Clothes*, was recognized as a readers' favorite in women's erotica by Romantic Times magazine. A full-time writer, Jaid lives in a cozy little village in the northeastern United States with her two children.

She welcomes mail from readers. You can write to her c/o of Ellora's Cave Publishing at P.O. Box 787, Hudson, Ohio 44236-0787.

COMING SOON:

ENCHAINED

An erotic bondage romance anthology

Death Row: The Mastering by Jaid Black
Mastered by Ann Jacobs
A Choice Of Masters by Joey W. Hill

Printed in the United States
1251600001B/33